Upon Reflection

Adam Spaven

Published in 2011 by New Generation Publishing

Copyright © Adam Spaven 2011

First Edition

www.newgenerationpublishing.info

INTRODUCTION

Before I start, I would like to ask you a question.

'Have you ever looked into a mirror and thought about or even asked yourself What if?'

I imagine that at some point , you yourself would of asked that very question. Not necessarily that exact question maybe with the alteration of , how? Why? When?. The possibilities are endless.

Such a simple device which takes light, creates an image then projects the parallel. With such simplicity yet it obtains the power to mend a broken heart if needed, or help you achieve your hopes and dreams. When the world seems to have turned its back on you, a mirror or any object reflecting your image will encourage strength as you still remain alive. Mostly preserving the vanity expressed in every small hole or matter of density. Vanity will no doubt be the end of humanity.

Returning back to the question set. Every time we ask ourselves leave for work, or the realms of socialization with colleagues or peers, use this object as a pinnacle of time along with importance to accomplish nothing. The mirror itself creating such an enigma of the idea that is a reflection of perfection in the mindset of the occupant that is reaching out. This feeling we exploit through every section of life makes us believe the tasks of accomplishment are achievable. However such an invention could produce a negative effect demising the personality into an introverted stasis protecting any emotional barrier.

This object in which we talk of will always remain to fulfil the task at hand. We as a race, the most dominant have no actual proven use for it, yet reflection is ever so important.

At a glimpse, one moment whether it's the start or finish, we see what we desire. One second may turn into a lifetime. That s definite, especially if every day you ask What if? Why? Or when?

The answer provided has multiple options itself. Does your reflection help you choose a path to walk or what you ask of it? Maybe they are nothing but merely rhetorical. A pinnacle of time wasted accomplishing

3

absolutely .... Nothing or maybe not.

I asked myself that very question that I asked you, providing myself with some unanswered questions and scenarios that I never thought I'd be in. The line between reality and imagination became so close to disappearing. Now I asked myself who or what am I? A mystery that will now be identified starting in the asylum.

CHAPTER ONE

Rocking backwards then forward, on a continuous basis whilst strapped in a white jacket restricting certain movements. In the corner of the room, looking towards a door. Would it be possible? Is it? The mental institution, an asylum or somewhere worse? That as a question is unviable. I certainly do not believe you. Prison maybe? No. Me, myself or I has done nothing wrong. A pillar of the community is what I am, therefore prison, ha throw that theory out of the window, any open door and especially the mind. Shouting at the peak of my voice to the point it began to hurt whilst disappearing at a slow rate. A sudden bang that is repeated with a voice on the other side shouting in response.

'Shut it Danny, You know what happened last time. You wouldn't want a repeat, but if you insist. It can be arranged.' Tears beginning to crawl down the uncertain face belonging to myself. At the time pale, Black eyes through the lack of sleep, with a rising bruise upon my cheek due to the constant throwing myself against the door as it was the only hard surface in the small isolated space enough to be described as a room.

On a continuous basis the rocking would not stop. Providing the comfort brought by the gentle motion of my mother rocking me in her arms as her first born. Speaking of mothers, the only possession at current would be the photo stuck upon the wall of course with sellotape nothing that could provide harm for example a thumb tack. Think a recent holiday. Definitely, it had to be. An image of perfection. Greatness it was, no better holiday in my life time so far. I miss her. With a life sentence, concealed in a padded box. What for you're thinking? Would you like to know? Ok, I'll tell you under the condition that you promise never to tell a soul. I said, you must promise not to tell a soul. Once again the rising voice taking over. A voice that will tell most of what he can remember with the belief he is a serial killer. Ok, thank you, let's begin. Well… Whispering with intent that nobody hears besides yourself. I killed two people, or was it more? With a cynical smile, repetition of my accomplishments so far would not be a far stretched tale purely through the enjoyment it fulfilled in me. The amount of joy provided was almost insatiable!! Hahaha...

'Ok, Danny, I warned you once. Nurse.' With the guard calling out for the assistance of the nurse.

The key turns, a bright light is all I see at this certain time with two dark shadows walking towards my direction. In front stands the guard holding his truncheon, the other figure an angelic beautiful creature that could certainly not be described at this moment in time.

'Ok, Danny this will not hurt,' she says in a feminine voice as a sharp prick becomes present in my neck.

Upon first appearances, through thinking that she was sent from the land that held the golden gates. Now it's shows she a messenger of death, the boat man waiting at the river Styx. Eyes slowly closing. After the insertion that was a sleeping sedative. The nurse cruelly placed the object without remorse, compassion and least of all sympathy.

Whilst sleeping it will be a lot easier to clear a few things up. The year is 2008. I have just recently being charged , tried and been given a life sentence without bail, with no get out of prison clauses. Face it. As a nation we all know the British legal system. Criminals would rather go to, or remain in prison. Far easier than remaining in the real world. Why? Good question, prison is free housing with three meals a day, again free of charge, well paid for through British taxes. Two hours a day which has such devices as the gym, internet access and a phone line. The real world that you have the comfort freedom would be described as the prison. Free is not as described in the dictionary. This expression can only be guaranteed with two things which are death as a certainty and the rise of taxes. Yet I am the one in the cell, please. At what point will you arrive to your senses? At least I do not have to work a minimum of forty hours a week to provide for myself and my family. Back to the issue,

A life sentence without any good behaviour clause. In the papers you read all the time that criminals are allowed are to roam free throughout the world as you call it. I am sure Bangkok is the new prison, a retirement home, a criminal institution providing the ultimate criminal fantasy or drugs, children followed with any abuse as they see fit. I heard that many former pop stars that end up there. I do not believe for one second that they are there to increase a tan line. My crime was murder. If you take my word as citizens they would not be referred as model. As parents I would advise that your children would be kept away from these that we speak. However a problem that over time as

6

been erased ha or executed haha! Again with the cynical laugh.

Yet I have still not explained the reasoning for the life sentence. Was multiple murder so bad? It will be described later to you all, the details , reasons for these wrong doings and finally the pleasantness provided in the performance of murder. A showcase with an easy five star rating! A film showing my past would not gain every detail.

Again with a smile. Through description it was one sided. Whilst rising in the one direction teeth starting to show. The smile of sarcasm in relation to that of a gangster getting his reward. A belief in which the devil, Satan, whatever you refer to him as would be very proud. A father which very soon we meet upon release or escape out of this damn jacket.

As I am in this unit does it automatically make me a very dangerous person? Were my killings the same as a serial killer? The stability of my mind out of sequence to the human body? Even murderers have rights. As reason this is no excuse to contain me in the asylum. Upon my voice raising then strapped down unwilling upon which I will be medicated to sleep. A complete copy of Hannibal Lecter's transportation from anywhere, completely retained. As expected a secured arrival in the transport vehicle. Well that was all in favour mainly in protection of the guards not myself or escape.

The trial itself is a confusion or mutiny as I believe all involved were far from neutral. The biased views of judge along with jury were present from the moment I entered that room. The eyes of people I had never encountered gleaming with pure hatred and discontent making me believe the decision had already been made. A conspiracy that would make sure I never walked alone again. The conclusion that I had clearly committed all crimes of which I was accused. The time I was about to waste defending myself just proves that the legal system is a mere fraud.

Once the introductions were made and everybody was accounted for. Realization entered my mind that without any competition all prosecutions are about to be placed upon me, without anyone to testify the claims. I sat accompanied by my attorney in appeal of crimes against myself, with only judge and jury in the courtroom. I always had the assumption that there had to be more than one party in a trial. An attorney who presented me had no remorse nor did he care if I was guilty or not, he was paid to represent and that was it.

The trial lasted a while as I recall, with the end of each day I was returned to a cell until the following day. Bail was a doubtful thought as the cost didn't justify any means plus I was under the assumption that I was innocent and it would be clear towards the ones who decide the outcome. Once I was arrested it was made clear, I was to remain under lock and key without bail until all decisions had been laid and recorded.

The attorney just kept rewording and rephrasing the judges testimony's trying to confuse the jury of the allegations. 'So Mr. Roberts, You claim that you have nothing to do with these crimes yet so far the defence given has far from proved anything. The evidence which has brought yourself here today and everyday this trial continues is stronger than the claims in which you make.' The judge made sure he was heard, a straight face supposedly unbiased without verdict.

'What evidence has been provided to this trial that makes my client guilty your honour? As I recall the evidence is all substantial and shows no real proof that my client was involved.' Strong remorseless words spoken by my representative. Taking a deep breath, looking around mainly at the jury considering the case returned back at him.

'Ok. I believe it time for a recess. I will ask that all the information upon this trial including all evidence to be renewed and processed. Court will be adjourned until tomorrow.' Banging down his hammer, as he stood all followed through respect along with courtroom procedure. Once he had left the room as did we.

A complete day had passed before court adjourned, allowing myself and legal representative to repeat or find any flaws within my testimony.

The judge insisted a legal representative was to speak in favour of the victims and prove the evidence placed myself as the one capable and guilty of the crimes in question. The evidence could not really prove I was guilty however small factors did not aid in any innocence either. The fight or bullying I was to encounter proved it was a presumed outcome, with no need to waste energy or even bother to fight back. So at this point it was down the opinion and verdict of the jury, whom of which had no intention of been involved let alone having to actually conclude a decision of which one man's fate was held.

Evidence against the word of mouth. Now it all became clear as the days followed guilt was all I was whether or not the pieces fit, there was no one else to commit to these acts so the verdict became clear.

Case closed, verdict guilty without question Court was over. Jail would now be the residence of this man. Would respect be more apparent or would it be a desirable quality to be earned over time or the reasons of which I'm accommodated? These were questions that lay within, as this environment was new to me.

If had been convicted of such horrific crimes why was it I had been placed in prison with a cell mate? I was an acclaimed serial killer with psychological issues and a danger to those around me. The sentence I would of posed, surely confinement away from others. Along with suicide watch at all times.

Within the retained memory according to certain flashbacks, I definitely had a cell mate. The person in which I speak proved himself not be very polite or an accepting person indeed, well that should not have been a surprise in the slightest, nobody in this hell hole was to be praised an angelic. He constantly referred to me as Barbie, the metaphor suggesting I would be a toy to play with. Through the induction process I was his personal bitch, well through his eyes anyway.

'This place you are in Barbie has an order to which at present has no space for your presence.'

'An order? There is an order you say. Are you top of this order? Or what place do you take? You speak down towards me in a condescending fashion as though you rule, would this be a true statement?' speaking back to the cell mate. Honestly I had yet to acquire any idea to his name. Truthfully it was no great loss or meaning in the back of my mind nor was I going to go out of my worthless way to find it.

'You dare mock me Barbie, ha! I pray to God you are not mocking me, were you mocking me?'

'I was not mocking anyone or intending to insult anybody. You spoke of an order which I presume is the position of authority amongst the inmates'

9

'Now you're taking the piss out of me. You don't believe me, that's why you're trying so hard to take the piss. Believe me Barbie it ain't going to work.'

Reaching the end of the sentence my cell mate showed me the reason as to why he was retained in this box of a hell hole.

One punch, two punch. Continuing to beat until blood began to expand every vein, artery or vessel that railed the blood within. Tears flowing like a water fall whilst the guard just stood observing as though a great West end musical was been performed for his entertainment .
Laughing, encouraging the beating to continue. Feeling like a life time of torture like all things it came to subtle end. The guard entered finally laughing, then kicking a wounded man only to observe to answer to a stupid question

'Am I alive?'

The slow breaths that struggled to escape the blocked tunnel that was my throat and mouth. Provided sufficient relief for a man who had no honour or care for his job. He turned leaving the cell singing in joy, after witnessing a crime in itself yet it was a far thought in his mind.

All I did was ask the simple question to find out who or what this man was sharing the cell in which occupied us both. Blood remaining on my face and clothes, he, my executor stood beside me. No beside me would suggest I had the ability of stance. This being stood over me casting himself purely as a shadow.

'Is order something you believe now or would another demonstration be required?' In a joyful fashion the cell mate spoke hoping for the latter question to be answered first.

'I have no desire nor do I care Barbie as to what you did out there. Honestly, truthfully I couldn't give a rat's arse as to who you are.' Without blinking, a set of eyes staring showing a frown upon his forehead providing a blurred scowl towards my direction elevating the point, making sure it sunk in. An excellent comparison would be a sulking child stamping their feet, crossing their arms in the local shop after mother refused a chocolate bar. When that angel turns demonic in a bid to gain what they believe is justice. That chocolate bar.

'Are we clear Barbie? It is a very simple question, are you retarded? Whether or not you are, it doesn't really matter. I would expect answer within seconds of asking. I apologize I am wrong with that statement. I would demand an answer.

Nodding was the easiest thing to do at the back of my mind. The remaining parts of my lifetime had to be spent with this joyful character. Provoking him at this point was far from an answer or alternative.

So there it was, weakened and truly beaten. Shortly after the pleasantries had past I discovered sleeping on the floor would be the resting ground in which I regenerate. This was a decision not made by choice upon my own accord. An option thrown upon myself, without compromise. The injustice that brought me to this place was multiple murders, the floor is no place for me. The ego alone has heightened itself upon a pedestal. The floor would emphasize stature of a rodent or insect not of a person who had been believing he was a ruler amongst men.

The fight or anger just wasn't in me yet. Respond or fight back? I wasn't drunk and I suppose he hadn't really motivated me. That sounds kind of silly. Look at the scenario in a simple light... the fire needs fuel to burn. So far all he done was place the wood forgetting to light the match!

Without a meal upon entry to the cell, requiring the energy to heal was running on empty let alone provide backlash. A time and place for everything would be the statement keeping down. Simply, found the cleanest unoccupied dark corner that would be free of urine or insects. A cell mate who actually allowed sleep with the mere reason he was not going to be distracted with my presence disturbing his nocturnal pattern.

CHAPTER TWO

Light becoming more apparent along with my sense's returning providing the use of my everyday bodily functions. Out of stasis I was drawn feeling like a whole lifetime had passed in such a small time frame. Curled up in the safety of comfort which was that bubble I lived in which only entertained myself. In any corner of choosing. Narrowing that down to four. One which remained still undisturbed apart from a minute puddle bathing the floor with a stench more potent than bleach however recognizable straight of the taste of aged urine sitting at the back of your throat. Body sore and battered not forgetting it had beaten down through the destruction of a yet to be named nemesis. Previous workouts at the gym could not compare to how I felt. Standing over casting his shadow, this is man who believed to be a great statue deserving praise for his accomplishment the night before. Wish I had such confidence!! Smiling as though Christmas morning had arrived early. Unwrapping every present under the tree, praying he had that toy on top of the list that got posted to Father Christmas. The blessing of a new cell mate. A man who was a virgin to this side of the legal system. Naïve as to what prison actually was, that honoured present on his list is how I appeared.

'Time for breakfast, Barbie,' A statement spoken as though the meal would be allowed to even approach my mouth let alone been rewarded grace to eat.

Standing there, breakfast came through the cell door. The guard different from yesterday passed me the tray.

'Barbie take a good look at your food, if your brain is capable enough then I suggest you take a picture. A subconscious Polaroid which will be the condition it arrived to you. Haha!' Smiling whilst chewing his own breakfast, observing my direction. Whilst spitting all contents every last piece that circled the inside of his mouth all over my tray making any of the food presented very quickly inedible. At this point I would say that dog food would be more desirable or even edible. Without choice it had to be eaten. Desperate times do call for desperate measures to maintain self-preservation, an energy source would be required. As far as I was concerned every meal could potentially be my last. I carried on. Saliva running all over this substantial meal. Liquid draining into every piece of whatever laid beneath it. Weakness and fatigue still set in. Nor had I completely regenerated enough to start a healing process. It had to be one or the other unless I ate. Never had I imagined that life could reach a standard of this level. If this was to be the first meal of the day I wondered as to how the others would be presented to me. The challenge to insist of how I intend to have a meal served was thrown out of the window the minute I lost that trial.

An interesting first day in prison. In which apparently I mocked my cell mate, found out I have a potential order which included the guards. Not an act of treason but most certainly there laid corruption amongst the guards. With a price unknown to me generating such power. The concerning issue that really these inmates had nothing to trade of value to a salaried employee. With order holding an unbreakable grip which spread amongst the cell mates. I understood, however the question upon this day how does this improve or prosper the guards? The respect shown towards myself was no greater than that shown towards the cockroach, whilst thinking it had more associates. A vision that clearly shows every time a cockroach made itself visible, it usually meant it's end, an inferior vermin that was to be banished upon sight. The ladder or order as it was known or told by every piece of crap circling this hell whole would certainly be in for a surprise. Tolerance or patience is only a strong point with the clear minded those who knew the art of suppressing unnecessary frustration. Dreaming whilst awake or asleep is a common factor amongst with every living mortal being. Personally mine sometimes a little far-fetched however if pursued in the right direction adding the formula of success then undoubtedly achievable. These inmates like myself dreamt of something providing that factor which may make allies or enemies only time would tell. Through a dream a personality could make an imprint or basis of a character.

The day that followed turned in a spiral of unforeseeable accounts not making my arrival better or pleasant. The meals had a repeating gravy of saliva which didn't improve taste. My strength slowly rebuilding not that it would make any difference. I was out numbered in a new environment. An enemy doesn't attack without knowing his opponent especially in unconquered ground. Access the situation then strike. I barely had knowledge of my cell and occupant let alone this order. A mass hunting ground which had untouched solitudes from this order as with whatever small glimpse I had of these in this section, were far from controlled by anyone. There is the possibility that they were the actual council of control. A ladder of respect with the density requiring the need of opinion through council. This place holding the lowest that mankind had to offer based itself upon structure through control, actually more organised than the outside. A neutral inmate had to exist somewhere within this asylum having similar thought of my cell mate. I could not be the only one, now time was on my side as it would allow me to find this person.

An unsuitable task of finding a person if one was to exist, in which they would aid in my shutting of a barbaric cell mate. It's not as though I may walk up to every prisoner and enquire about this man without consequence placed upon my head. Offending a possible life partner as better way to describe our relationship could not be an option at this moment. How? A revelation will happen just unaware of the how.

Later that morning shower time approached. A glamorous tail of possible stereotype however the truth of silenced confinement had to be told. A small piece of soap that was provided by the guard. Still weak, nervous of the next encounter. The order may become clear, control through rank could possibly allow myself with personal hygiene. The order may just to be this section, or it may extend throughout the whole prison. The anxiety caused subtle shaking when holding objects no matter shape or size.

Once wet it quickly slipped ejecting as a missile through the hands in which it was contained. Again contained in a room, tiled surface known amongst in the inmates as the bathroom where the showers were to be found. I say it like that as it reminded me of the showers at school, dark covered in dark growing damp surrounding the corners spreading along the rim of the block. Bad luck showed itself only this time through circumstance greater than the initial greeting made upon my entrance. The cell mate in the next shower area proved himself to be my cellmate. Coincidence or factual truth that this is how shower time took place. Him along with two others glaring in the direction that showed the image of my naked body with water running all over. The beginning to an erotic sensation to these three. A sick thought to some, maybe fantasy to the rest however it will remain as truth to me.

'You dropped your soap Barbie? I'm thinking that I help you by picking it up and giving it back! No. I'd rather you pick it up as I owe you nothing let alone such a simple task. It has to be picked up Barbie otherwise the cleaning you desire along with very much required will be very hard!! YEAH!! I like that idea.' slapping the chest of a member of a nearby colleague associate or possibly a lower ranking part of the

14

order. He returned the gesture with a laugh along with nodding his head as though he had no choice of the matter.

THE ORDER was without doubt the largest entity within in these walls. Life controlled by rank along with word. A clear representation of the political government that dominates the lives of so many. Two of the three pushed the centre of my chest knocking me straight to the floor below. I wish I had slipped along the wet surface as the pain inflicted would have been quick and over briefly without a reminder of a man's hand print amplified by the water. The floor I lay counting two variations of pain. Within seconds those two knelt beside me forcing their own weight which forced my shoulders to remain as they landed. Without a say or opinion I had to remain beneath two stronger structures than myself. In comparison to that of the guard as the nurse treated a patient whilst installing the sedative.

Like a piece of new raw fresh meat. My personal cell mate once satisfied with the restraint held upon me came down to floor, kneeling as close as possible. He placed the palm of his hand upon my forehead gently circling his thumb up around my nose, chin wherever along the circumference of my face it followed. Inhaling a deep breath making sure his eyes always focused directly into my eyes, and thoughts. Softly kissing the lips whilst the shower ran over all of us. Smiling after the kiss was over.

'The cleanest kiss you'll receive, past, present or future Barbie! Honestly the gentlest I ever kissed anyone so far. Ever since your arrival you just keep bringing forward urges providing me with senses, emotions and passion. I feel that the formalities are over and introductions are complete. The essentiality to fulfil my internal insatiable needs held over has reached its pinnacle. You definitely deserve this treat I am about to lay upon you, oh yes. Needing such passion for a cause can only make you ejaculate a well, I can tell you desire it as much as I. It's just going to be a little painful at first like a virgin in which you are at this stage. That will pass as the sensations increase's releasing passion the closer I reach your g-spot but hopefully not so quick. On an even more positive note Barbie, this thrill you will receive and come to love as much as every man in here. Multiple times over in which a guarantee you would never get at home. Haha!! No woman could provide this on coming gift, please enjoy and appreciate, Ok! Turn him over, now I'm ready. Come On. NOW.' Spoken whilst his voice erected into a very sudden shout. Whilst ordering his minions he started to rub, following a playful motion of his penis. The more he played the larger it grew. It now became more obvious to me as the blood rushed to his penis making it completely erect. Following his speech about emotion and feeling, this would be another part of the induction process providing joy towards him. Now to become a sexual dummy.

Still the shower time with a never approaching end the cell mate using the water as a lubricant. Starting with the hands, just caressing and circling the rim towards the passage trying to provide a sensation maybe a smile upon my face. However that as a crime itself reached a thankful end, maybe the whole situation. Luck was not on my side, nor would prayer help. Forcing himself upon me, thrusting his hips through me, through the space that no man should allow passage in that direction. Multiple times which continued to get harder yet slower so he would get the pleasure in which he sought without a brief ending. The clarity that the shower would wash away any remains of the act. After finishing his sexual needs that were fulfilled through me then the other two took their place treating me as a sexual dummy found in an adult shop. The dice were rolled, the pawn I became to pleasure these sick individuals at certain intervals. Thankfully shower time came to an end. Laying on the floor in complete pain bleeding once again. However in a place that never crossed my mind would draw blood. Slowly been washed away turning from a dark gothic red to a very pale pink as it exited through the drains. My blood was lucky after one day it already found an escape. Why could I not be so fortunate?

Meal time was now to be accompanied with the shower creating tears to be greater than the previous shower. Where was the aid to help, anyone? Why would nobody come to my rescue? The prevention needed so the pain would never had started let alone be felt. After the assault or rape in which it be known through the legal system. The guards would not touch me. The remaining inmates walked past laughing in joy as though there time as a toy is over. They would certainly not go backwards to help me now they are essentially free from the pain. Gently but firmly, even as quick as I could stumbling towards my feet. Slipping once or twice, eventually stability was achieved. Still bleeding though.

Order. Ok, Order will be achieved and presented however not towards myself nor would I be the representative to teach it. The man that supposedly took my virginity will soon at some point impose his will upon any one let alone myself. Innocence was a small piece of this body that remained intact, now belonging to him. Without fair it was stolen not asked for just taken without consent, how unjust this action was. Exits are created for the one purpose. It is not to be used as an entrance to speed up the impatience of a man's sexual need. Like the single men in the world, masturbation would be a suitable answer not rape.

Through the acquaintance of a meeting that went wrong they have formally in every dimension been introduced to this body on two levels. Time has no meaning or thought to myself now. A continuous cycle of numbers that simply laid resting upon a device. Which I would rarely see, let alone visualize. So the clock needn't bother as I had plenty. Not as though I was going anywhere. Shall the voices that lay deep within the mind controlling this body be released. Through generosity those words spoken to me kindly provided the shelter that would turn out to be place of my current residence. Demonic is the best fitting description of one of the voices. In which pure evil resigns however I believe it's one of many that speak but that is yet to be proven as its always sounds the same. On this I guarantee, vengeance shall be accomplished without any remorse.

The Order. Who is the actual leader? Thankfully to speed up things there he stood with his cynical smile, happy achievement that gained some very required urges to be settled. My cell mate was the leader. How coincidental!! How grateful I became.

'Hey Barbie, enjoy the ride this morning? Not too painful I hope? Ha! It made a smile show upon my face. The smile nearly reached the eyes. Yes!' Barbie that God damn name again, He refers to myself as Barbie.
In reference as to what Barbie is, a dim blonde made of plastic who lacks intelligence. Stereotyping that people who have blonde hair posses the same traits and similarities.

'Why do you keep calling me that? Do you have a purpose for it or reason behind the cause?'

'Hahahaha! Does it piss you off?' laughing just continuing, it was becoming a very quick hobby as to his progression was easily achieved.

One, last final mistake. Which soon would be his last. Standing face to face with a nameless criminal due to the fact I never asked therefore no reason to learn. For the first time, the spitting came from the direction of my mouth, containing my saliva. Amusement brought a smile to my actual face however this time anger reached the cellmate.

'Before you react to the previous action, at least think of the consequence. Do you know as to why my presence stands before you in this cell, in the prison?' Time stood still. Blacking out. Yet, still waking besides my cell mate. We were both on the floor. Strange. He always slept in his bed with what little comfort it provided. I remember spitting in his face then I woke. Confusion had taken over. Worry eating away at me as to proceedings of the in-between.

Yet I woke to see him lay bleeding from the mouth, dribbling down his chin creating a puddle beneath the face. The neck snapped in such a primitive fashion it could be turned or lifted in any direction without difficulty. The agility as to the neck it always fell towards the floor with an attraction to gravity. Clothes removed including underwear. This was not removed off the body completely with it remaining upon the person we speak of. The underwear was rammed straight to the back of his mouth blocking any oxygen to enter or exit, one lesson taught. Exits and entrances serve their own purpose. Luckily this underwear also prevented any screams to hail the guard. Now no one else had the ability to rescue with every door locking the same way. Whilst beating the excuse of a human he was, a piece of crap in better terms it extended one step further causing certain breaking points. Now the frustration with this man had reached beyond its means pushing my mind out of order. This maybe premeditated, not sure on that one. Preventing screams with an echo the thought came to me. The moments leading up to his death were actually created by myself releasing the sexual urges a man builds up. Once the orgasm came which was released across as much of the body as physically possible. Boredom set allowing me to break the neck. The joy. Could you imagine it? The scenario is very much possible, without feeling weird towards me let's continue on.

Upon arrival in hell, the reaper I believe would turn him away, however where would he go? The positive from his death is one less scumbag to ever be released. His crime would be far the last thing he'll remember wherever he ends up. My face with the torture supplied and the sacrifice I made of him in his final hour.

18

Oh dear, a slight error of judgement has been made. Murdering him should not of occurred. Think of the pain that could have been passed upon one over a long period of time. He also was persecuted to remain in this cell, going to any guard claiming he was been bullied would not look good towards his reputation. I also believe the guard would far from accompany the needs of his claims and relocate to different cell to accommodate his comfort.

Stress levels are reached upon us all, causing myself to crack upon three days of pain brought to me. Bullying by anything will not be accepted. For the past, present and obviously the future arriving day by day, Royalty should be the status crowned towards me. An insect who could be stood on! Not going to happen. Walking in to the cell upon the morning in which we have been speaking of bringing breakfast. With one foot in through the door, trying to gain sight of both of us. Movement only shown by myself. Swiftly looking at the cellmate seeing the damage caused towards one person with only myself been in the room, the truncheon raised in such a fashion a record could have been broken!! Alerting his partner shouting

'Raise the alarm, NOW.' within seconds the prison went back to lock down. The truncheon swung towards my skull without time to react, it was quick enough to put me in isolation. All I had done was wake up.

Alone. There I sat in complete darkness. I presumed far too much from this place. Killing in prison is still frowned upon and apparently still illegal. Shocking! Days into a life sentence with routine showing its ugly grip over the mind which controls me. Not allowing a rehab to begin, once it started to show then it took over, a beginning towards a pilot episode that would end. Finding that in prison, isolation prevents the harm of any other human being. Would I never have believed that honour does exist amongst thieves without catching a glimpse of it myself.

Society upon appearance is different to every factor. Humble upstanding members of society have law and order to follow. Agreeing to policy set whether you believe it to be right or wrong. Please remember the line if I have taught you nothing then remember this DON'T TRUST NO ONE (D.T.A) as they do not trust you. Everyone is out to gain an individual purpose or motive for themselves. Selfish Bastards. Everyone.

Sitting in solitude without any sound. The only sound heard was that made by myself. Not the best way to punish anyone really. If depression set in whilst free and at home. I would find myself at the pub sat in the corner drinking. Watching, admiring the people around me thinking are their lives any worse or better than mine. What's changed apart from the lack of beer and view of a middle class man?

Deserving to be here, in this room. The blackout leading to the pair of us lay on the floor is far from explanation at this point.

Before been caught, I was at Sarah's just simply watching TV. Ten minutes into this activity boredom set amongst the two of us. Making out, sweet soft kissing came as natural process as though it was meant to happen, with chemistry between us both. Just as quick as we started, the clothes began peeling off one another.

The bedroom became a place of hot passion. Sarah's figure compared to that of a super model if not better especially through my eyes'. A flat stomach, a tight petite arse that simply shone beauty. Sarah had a really low self esteem, making the transition between us far easier to manipulate to suit my sexual requirements.

  'Do you have it?' the smile reflected through this beauties eyes alone.

  'Yeah, of course. Are you ready for some pleasure?' a reply made by myself.

A condom was not what she was referring to. The gram of coke that lay dormant, idle at the bottom of the pocket in my trousers which lay on floor. She insisted that she wanted her line made on the bedside cabinet. Who was I to argue? Taking a credit card out of my wallet to aid in the process of making this thrill factor. After the line was made I found an old receipt which making use of as well as recycling I rolled into a tube. Her line sat along the bedside cabinet, now ready for her taking. I stood back viewing as she snorted the line. Hearing that extended sniff, providing such a beautiful smile. Now her high had been achieved, it was only fair that I had my turn. Meaning the thrill of the coke and ride she would provide. Where to start? Easy, throw her flat on her back. Pull down her black lace knickers, revealing a clean shaven pussy making it easier to set up the two lines. It would have been far too messy if remained untrimmed in any sense of the word. I had now begun the next stage of love making for us both. Whilst down there might as well start with the tongue, creating screams of joy. Leading to the process of fucking which included handcuffs, vodka and something else. Fuck's knows! However boredom set in. Calling a taxi to go home oh well she most certainly had a smile. Waking up the following morning or whenever it was with a banging headache. Far greater pain exceeded than that of a hangover. Could not of been the vodka, I'll just not have that next time.

Speaking of that memory it remained the nearest, closest feeling as to my particular mood now. That erotic time with Sarah had no comparison, it was definitely far better. A girl allowed me to enter with consent followed by an empowering force which grew upon us both. Inside a man! Hardly, that same erotica provided by Sarah. It would never be replicated by any male. A lifetime in prison, choice may not be an option, it may have to be take what you can, whenever possible.

CHAPTER THREE

Still how does this convicted felon end up in the mental part of Parkhurst prison which is supposedly the worst in the country? Performing such acts to other people in confined spaces got me a week in isolation. Upon release after this week things took a turn for the worst. There was no order; the rule is you show respect towards the long timers. Not kill them upon arrival. Without the explanation of how here came to be. Attention brought to me by these inmates was overwhelming. Feedback provided, some good and the rest is self-explanatory. Desiring ultimate respect off all these creatures for some unknown reason, something had to be done. Open to suggestions?

Fortunately an idea came to mind. More an epiphany. Requiring the assistance of the guard the one that stood over me whilst been beaten. It just made no sense as to why I was retained in a straight jacket. Freedom at present became more a fantasy.

Paper work showed the reasoning as to why I am here. The guard doubtfully red it, as far as it concerned him this inmate is a number joining the chain. The legal system placed myself on a pedestal naming me as one of the worst killers ever known. Through brutality and fashion of the accomplishment created by premeditation would place a label on any soon to be criminal, well at the back my subconscious mind anyway. Stupidity soon came to show its self from the guard's perspective as he had the cheek to ask me.

'What you in for, Fraud!! Yeah, can't see you doing anything else. Fraud I think even that is a little farfetched.'

'Oh no no no! You just did not imply that. I was under the impression that you read my file. Maybe the big words exceeded your intelligence at an extraordinary pace. This was probably the reason to his mother providing such a simple name. Can't struggle with simplicity. It would surely highlight my crimes. Stupid is a compliment to you I think.'

'No, dickhead I read your name, and length of time that I have to look at your really fucked up face. I couldn't give a shit what you're in for. Your one less piece of shit off the street as far as I'm concerned.'

Imagining his thoughts, whilst he pronounced those words. The crime would be directly below my name, if not highlighted on my file, if he has actually taken the time to read it. The more he spoke, the more it became apparent he had not. He was given my name by a colleague. That was all he needed to know. Through that lack of laziness it proved this man's ignorance. This was already beginning to agitate me.

Committing fraud. How do you do start the process of the crime he just implied. I would not know where to begin. With a face only a mother could love, in fairness she must have put a blanket over, purely to make her life more joyful. Turning towards that direction to make sure he saw the reply leave my mouth.

'Murder you stupid ignorant bastard. Since been here I have already committed one. Would you like to be number two?' Cynically smiling, reflecting my thinking at that time. Unfortunately it was a rhetorical question, even if it was to be literal, it would be far from grasp.

Murderers as a stereotype tend to show no emotion in any sense of the word. Dead inside allowing pain to be mindset. Guards that retarded have no right asking such silly question's with the cheek to imply fraud was my undoing. That fuse snapped once again. That hour glass had once again been turned at the back of my mind. Time was ticking, however it was waiting for... Hurt provided pain ruining or lowering the only pride remaining in this shell of a body. All by a dumb, fucked up, retarded guard. Death being a certain within life. Well I guarantee death was surely about to knock on the guards door.

I speak as though it would be impossible. Everything is possible. Find your goal, centre it then work round it constantly reminding yourself of the intention. Always remain focused on the target, never rush however seek the opportunity as it will not come to you very often. Once the foundations are laid, find the cracks, the weaknesses and hurdles that may stop you. Sort them, remind yourself of the focus, sort out the equipment, pay your dues. Replay the whole thing as a scenario from both positive and negative outcomes. Once all has been accomplished and you're satisfied with the product, then reach for the opportunity creating the possibility and outcome you desire. If you rush the design, thinking without patience it is most likely you will fail as you are thinking past the focus more of yourself. Now I have work to do. A guard as dishonoured myself through his words. Time he learnt, everyone is equal.

Would you like to hear the story of how the guard met his own demise? Prison had the similarities of a car boot sale. Whatever you desire or want, it will be sat in front of you. Price dependant on product would make a recession seem pleasant. Rasta known amongst his peers was the man to see. A shop keeper as such. Playing cards at a table, the game they played I was unsure of. Around him but not close joining in the game were his peers and maybe friends if they existed. Another description would be bodyguards as an entourage. Approaching the table all stood apart from Rasta. Providing a signal so the guards did not approach the table, he coughed a few times. Very cloak and dagger!!

'Who the hell are you man?' In hysterics whilst asking the question.

'Danny, Danny Roberts, Are you Rasta?' a simple reply.

'Danny, Danny who? Am I meant to care that you are Danny Roberts.' not so much the pleasant reply I was expecting.

'I came to seek yourself, my name need not be of any importance.' Standing tall as though I was the bigger man involved amongst this conversation.

'You seek, Rasta. You approach this table without any concern, you have the cheek to interrupt our game in which I was about to win. Yet you have no intention of explaining who you are. I will tell you something absolutely free of charge'

I stood before him in patience interrupting his speech. 'What?'

'Stop wasting my time; turn your white arse around and crawl back to which ever cell you belong. A word of advice Danny Roberts don't bother me again.' Conversation over, well he thought it had come to an end.

'I seek you, I waste my free time yet you have the nerve to treat me ever so rudely. That whoever you are is very disrespectful. There is no need to react like that, and then hide behind whoever this lot are.'

'Now your been rude Mr. Roberts. I have told you to piss off. Now heed my words and go. I don't care who you are, now fuck off I'm

24

busy.'

Inhaling a deep breath without any of my body moving an inch. I showed no fear. Any part of the current situation could and will be solved. Remaining calm trying not to react unnecessarily that may cause more damage on my behalf.

'You need my name? Roberts, Daniel 'Danny' Roberts is how I was christened. Now you know. I will gladly leave you to your childish humour.' Standing up from the chair below. Turning to walk away.

The laughing soon came to an end, his face went cold, a glare became apparent. His arm reached forward making sure I saw.

'You're The Game?' I stood still without answer or reaction.

'Yeah you are, I thought you were a myth. I have heard your name. Just never thought you were here. Sit, join us, please.' The glare kept in his eyes showing the mistrust. Maybe a little upset he disrespected me before knowing who I was. That we will never find out.

Through Jamaican decent was Rasta, he was raised in a small part of Stockport, known as Redish. I would not raise a rat in this place it would be unfair for the creature. The whole area could be compared to Beirut. A crumbling, deserted war zone occupied by the lowest uncaring people in Stockport. A mass council estate which was never improved just left as a detracting wasteland. The poor just thrown into it, the middle class avoided it. The job centre just signed that jobseekers allowance when there address appeared. It was clear the people from Redish never had the intent to job search, still they got paid from the taxes. Our taxes.

Rasta had long, thick dreadlocks. A gold tooth accompanied with the build of a brick wall. As order did not rule as first thought, this section of prison was definitely governed by him. No evidence to prove this claim just the weariness shown from the surrounding elements. Even the guards held their distance. The respect shown towards this man was greater than that placed upon my former cell mate.

Prices set by this man were certainly far from cheap; however a confined, concealed prison with demand for the unattainable had to be high. A simple philosophy in business, states that you buy cheap sell high. Profit is any entrepreneur's goal. At present that was no concern. The price set and paid by myself.

'How may I help you?' to start the conversation, through his ear my response came in a whisper.

Choice brought confusion to the face of Rasta in which he pondered as to what was just asked of him. He nodded his head although I think that was because the game of cards which continued through our talk was just won by him.

'Dude you are seriously fucked up.' The toy requested was there, Miracles were soon to be performed. Rasta pushed his dreadlocks aside, looked at both myself and the toy then walked away. Simple. Why can't all business be this simple? Order, Pay, Receive, Enjoy the merits.

The toy had arrived, to set up very simple. Execution will occur at breakfast, as metaphor the last supper, haha! Sorry my bad. A dish best served cold would be revenge! Breakfast was no full English. Shame really, I had not had fried bread or black pudding in a long time! Lay in silence, waiting to achieve a goal. Without sleep, the night was not apparent as it did not matter. Rocking once again, back and forth causing severe frustration. Which lead to pacing through the cell, creating a crater in the cell floor. Patience boiled into agitation, almost anger. Adrenaline surging throughout my veins, for example: A boy racer driving his toy (Subaru Impreza for example) as fast as it will go down that straight road, with the urge to push the N.O.S button. This one button provided ten seconds of rippling adrenaline surges. If done wrong may lead to certain death. Click, the lock began making its sound. Slowly but surely the door began to open. Ready to pounce upon the target, something was wrong. A different guard walked through the passage. Where is the other one? The special retarded case of a guard.

'Tony? Nah Tony is not in till next week, shift change. Why you want to murder him as well? Ha, Come on Danny breakfast time. 'Retard had a name, what a shock.

His name was of no meaning to me, however it serves a purpose as upon arrival it can be asked. This new guard seemed to know who I was, and through surprise to myself did not attempt to treat me like a piece of crap. Did politeness have meaning? Confusion it brought as the question would not be answered in my head. I have to know. After breakfast the question was asked.

'Why do you treat me humanely? Within a degree of normality. Well with the exception of these chains.'

Laughter was exhaled before his response.

'Well Danny you are here for life, as much it feels like for me twenty years. It's far too long for two people to hate each other or not get along. You agree?' He made sense, speechless I became looking straight through or even at him.

He only treated me with respect to gain his own personal needs and agenda in comparison to any man. Twenty years as a relationship to describe it, he gained my respect that morning. Time was endless when I get out of bed! To claim his pension through early retirement would be a fair assumption. The shift change meant they switched wards or had a day off to switch either morning or nights upon the Rota. He has to return. I have chosen his end acting as representative of the grim reaper, Tony needs to catch the boat at the time I set.

One week later a bang upon the door.

'Danny get up, Now Danny.' Yes he'd returned to me. Wow! There is a God!

Should I kill him now? The unknowingly prey in front of me which could now end the waiting. No, allow one more day with the reason to increase the hatred within. Playing the chess game, been his pawn waiting for checkmate! With a song providing entrance to the alter ego from the subconscious region of the mind began to play. A true rock band wrote this trophy playing through my mind. Head Motor. The title was Game Time. One pounding guitar riff starts the tune. Strumming one of the easiest chords. Motivating, is the best way to describe it.

'Time to play The Game, pause, time to play the game, hahaha, guitar once again, bang... It's all about the game, are you playing? It's all about control and are you taking? It's all about debt and can you pay it?' with it continuing on a loop in my mind.

Motive, right there in front of me, the subject nearly ready, soon to be in place. This song playing pushing me to believe I am a Game, not to

27

be played.

Keeping the ego within me present, close towards the surface yet far enough away to inflict harm at that moment. The song was always sung out loud during every kill. Drawing closer as time now was an element as waiting for the prey to enter. Excitement just made it hard to bear the wait. Straight faced unlike all the other kills. This was different. The kill had an unexpected element that weapons were an impossible factor with the belief that the guard had the power. How? With just a stick and an alarm to bring more. Well that was out of the question if someone just happened to be on the floor. The outcome would be certain, the plan always in my head due to fact I had nothing else to think about. If a task is to be performed at least do it properly to its full potential.

Shift change was nearly due with the guards talking about it been only an hour away making the time roughly five am. A basic formatted Rota, Six-two, Two - ten, Ten - six. Unsure how, Tony always appeared through the morning shift, without even doing another shift. Unless management was his role, that could be the only explanation. When I worked, it was the only way I managed to get away with it. Manager, Tony, not buying it! If killed would it make him a martyr? That is not going to happen. Through this man my pride tented, he hurt my feelings. Eye's opening to their full expansion, the song beginning; choice was no factor, control slipping out of my fingers. Welcome the alter ego, welcome The Game. Someone was due to die within minutes or hours. Martyr? Not a chance. You treat an animal with a whip it will surely attack. Imagine the scene if he treated myself badly, who else was on that list showing now respect to anyone. Haha!!

Lifting that table of a bed in search of. Yes you guessed it! My new toy! One arm extended outwards, reaching for that toy provided by Rasta. To kill with bear fist's a little out of reach even for me. Providing myself with a weapon, aiding in the execution. Using a pillow case off the bed, I started to polish it. Any sin created previously disappearing slowly but surely, this had to be done as Rasta did not explain how or where it came from.

Louder and louder the song sung. Tony's time approached. His shift closing in. I hope he's prepared to meet an unexpected guest. Shining reflected in comparison with that of a mirror. Silence covered the walls and housing of the corridor as six became the time. It may have been shift change yet I was still no closer to my prey, I was still sat in wait.

Breakfast is served at eight. Two hours to go, allowing myself to renter what was mine. Falling into motion swiftly. Bang on the door.

'Get up Danny,' Just as before. Without grace or compassion it was clear that Tony was back on shift. Abrupt has his awaking was, I imagine it was consistent with every cell mate. A repetition of banging. Followed by the simple speech just altering the name. A true drone. Yet this was still no reason for the way he treated myself once within my presence. At arm's reach but hidden under the protection of a brick wall that was my former inmate. This time he had no such barrier.

I forgot to mention, shadows could be seen through a small window allowing me to hide the weapon. In a square domain a weapon could be hidden anywhere as to the guards they were impossible to gain. Therefore lead to the ignorance that weapons could not harm them as they don't exist. A weapon could be anything from a paperclip to a gun. If the executor has a plan for an object to be included with slight improvisation then so it shall be.

Tony did not think I was capable of murder until our last encounter which I believe he still thinks was my mistake, maybe pure luck on my side. Not this time. The format in place, the plan drawn up now to execute!

CHAPTER FOUR

Walking through the opening door, the song reached a peak of loudness.

'Time to play The Game.' Closing any sanity left within myself. Once again as it approached, I blacked out. To the point brought forward so far, please a lame excuse as such as blacking out.

Now I will introduce myself. You may call me The Game. My presence has formally been introduced as well as the honour I'm now here amongst you. Perfection is in front of you as that of a God. Every man, woman even child on the planet is graced with an alter ego if not many. If say you're going on a night out, it may show through the mirror bringing forward confidence or arrogance to shield you, as makeup is applied, your hair altered from a daily basis. So much effort. What for? A few hours to impress one and other?

Well, Danny by others would be described a sad, lonely, depressed excuse of a man. He can't even throw a punch as he hits like a little girl! Important decisions have never been answered through him, too improve his life when asked to make a decision I'm brought forward. Simplicity is not as how I describe it, there is a clause. Dependency was the way it became as Danny drew weaker. Through this element I took control, telling him when I want to see the world it shall happen without choice. Relationship is a joint effort supposedly. This marriage I wear the pants. Haha! I'm good.

The cell mate was a wanker. That's it nothing more to say about that. At this point Danny would normally apologize for the use of foul language. Remember I'm not Danny. Why should I say sorry? Danny had the common tendency to back down from a confrontation always allowing defeat. That just is not acceptable. As before I take control, make me say no. I need to clear a little thing up, a small description is needed of how that cell mate met his end.

To provide an allowed distraction I spat straight into his eyes. Kneeing him right in the balls. That is a great feeling, watching another man fall towards myself. Grabbing hold of his narrow minded little head, whilst it received a present in the shape of my knee. Honestly it was beautiful, straight to the nose. Upon arrival it broke instantly. He placed one hand on his chin. Shortly after, he managed to push himself upwards onto his unsteady feet. The other hand placed on the forehead. Now perfection is an important factor now. Holding tight on the forehead whilst it was too forced towards the ground keeping the chin in the same place. A beautiful sound which could be described as the neck snapped, honestly you should have been there. It had to be done again, so it was repeated over and over until it just refused to make a sound. It soon became lymph with every movement. It just kept rolling towards the ground. Dead he maybe however Satisfaction still not quite there in my eyes. I removed his clothes until he lay in front of me naked. I could not tell you why but I asked the question.

'Do you dare call me Barbie now?' even upon completion, satisfaction had yet arrived. He received a kick, with the fact I expected an answer. Something needed to be done otherwise Danny would have shown his pathetic self.

Sifting through the clothes as they came off his back picking at certain items. Once I found his boxer shorts I screwed them into a tight packed little ball. I shoved them straight down his throat allowing a part to remain at the mouth. I had mentioned previously that it was to prevent screams, well I lied. The dead do not make sounds. Without a weapon I had just killed with bare hands. Nothing has that simplicity, what I have I missed. I will let you know when I discover it. I'm nearly perfect as a trained or celebrated Marine, Green Beret or the S.A.S just remaining in as host with no future. Straightening his arms then cracking at the elbows. It's a celebratory win of a game. Thinking, fuck it! Finish it. Making sure it was flat in a straight position on the floor, then I jumped into the air landing with a knee driving itself with such force upon the chest. Impact creating multiple breaks of the rib cage. One bone is all it takes to puncture at least one lung. Boredom set in quite rapidly. Looking down the rest of the naked body within my grasp, an arousing feeling came to me. Turned him over, removed my pants, with my erection it simply got shoved straight up his rectum. Over and over again, multiple times, through great force throughout the continuation until ejaculation occurred. Upon arriving at the gates of hell. How beautiful a reminder of his worthless final hour on earth?

I'm sure Danny described that sexual act as though his was alive. No! It would bring unnecessary risk of a guard approaching the cell, if a noise became heard. Plus I prefer him dead. More of an arousing turns on showing a remarkable control over his weakness increasing throughout

31

my dominance. It would never of happened if he just left me alone, not raping me and the Barbie thing just a little too far through my eyes. The situation could not continue. Therefore I put an end to it. Are acts of sexual conduct needed along with death, your asking do I kill to replace sexual urges? Is there something missing whilst having sex? I would not know. All this related to lust brings to mind those five seconds before any killing there is an insatiable feeling. This just takes you to ascension, no greater feeling describes it. It maybe that your right however just keep this in this mind, I'm me not you and you are certainly not my therapist. I am describing an unpleasant time in my life, not under analysis. Let's return to the story.

Upon finishing the sexual act, Danny took back over allowing me to return to where ever it is that I belong. I am nice guy, that I lay next to the body allowing the exchange between Danny and myself to occur through sleep. This was like a present to Danny with a big surprise of a dead raped cell mate. The game was over, we won, the score one nil. People need to learn very quickly I am here for a reason, without any doubt obviously.

Second game of the season is about to begin. Where we up to so far? Danny blacked out of course, providing time for myself to make my presence known. One thing first before we begin. Did Danny ever mention the weapon choice that he was polishing for me? It was not a gun nor was it a knife. The reason behind Rasta calling me fucked up. My weapon of choice was a sledge hammer. Hahaha!!! The memories brought back through this simple tool, provided great joy with happiness. The headless horseman had the sword. Hitler had an armada along with the gas chamber. I just use the tool used amongst builders and those within the trade. Ironic, men use it to build where as I use it to destroy.

We know the song was at maximum, the light became greater as Tony walked through the door entering my space, with a smile at Tony.

'Morning Tony, You ok? Time has ran out, your battery is dead as shortly as you will be. Hahaha!!!!'

Tony stood before me, eyes maximized in every direction looking in fear right at my face without choice, my eyes. He knew that escaping fate or destiny at this point, now impossible or did he just shit his pants? As he stood there before me, I had to ask.

32

'Any last words... haha!!' From behind my back the perfectly polished head of the hammer came across my nose covering most of my face with the smile still showing.

His arm rose with one finger pointing at the hammer.

'How...How did you get that?' breathless he became with fear turning his face a very pale white. Whilst trying to walk backwards, just unable too.

Fuck it, Lunging forward throwing the hammer head gliding naturally through motion, went straight into his eyes and forehead. The power exerted lead to a crack. Gravity pulled the hammer straight towards the floor whilst still on ever gracing Tony's face. Gravity a force I wish to control. Poetic motion as his head just bounced off the floor. The hit would not kill, I'm not going to allow that. Standing over my victim I looked down. But first I shut the door.

'You should of respected me Tony! Nothing hard I ask of you. Deserving last words is far from your reach. Now I am the guard! And you, you are my bitch!'

Straight towards his head the hammer fell. The stick in which made the hammer so great, providing that extra leverage required was right before my face once again. Poor adrenaline sent my shoulders flying towards Tony. His larynx spat blood everywhere throughout the cell as the hammer head hit. This blood incursion included my face. It dribbled down my face, towards my lips allowing me to reach out, to provide an erotic sensation as I tasted it, believe me it was good!! Similar taste to that of a Starbucks coffee. I suppose it was fair trade! Hahaha!

Once again rising the sledge hammer now it was swung as though it was a nine iron golf club. His neck was snapped through the great force expelled. Bringing myself once again to move with the memento carried, what a tremendous feeling. Standing over him in the same way the larynx was destroyed. It brought the idea to break the sternum. This killing was just getting better and better. So performing the same task, I broke the sack which contains the testicles. I think I became breathless, should of done that first, shame!

Without warning the other guard ran through the door, time was a factor on the outside. Tony had been gone too long. The arrival was far too late. A system that should protect these work colleges as a team or dare I even suggests friendship. Reliance upon each other, down to the very last man not the biggest factor, as clearly shown. Looking upon my result the guard that ran tried to take control of the situation by swinging that dam truncheon in my direction. Missing his target which was I, it just pissed me off whilst crossing the line. Before the action taken I held no grudge. Did he want to join in? Make him game three or just the second half of this game. It was bound to become difficult. To kill again especially for no reason was not why I killed. But did he swing at me? Yeah decision made, I'm happy to play again.

Sarcasm showed it had a lovely smile once again. Swinging his little truncheon in comparison to the hammer right towards me, I took the step back so he missed. Now my turn, the hammer went straight in the direction of the knee caps. Remembering now he'll never walk again. Such a shame! All this occurring before breakfast. Wow! Oh, I forgot to mention I swung the hammer through his stomach as he lay on the floor. Crying like a little baby. Wondering what was for breakfast! Think it will be the same as yesterday. That was it, once again cereal! As you'd imagine the second guard was no Tony!! Just a little toy to make check mate once again. I won't go into the same detail as before but to finish the game in play, I raped this one. I made sure the door was shut!! With his mouth filled with his own boxers. This bastard interrupted my kill, so he just had to pay a price. The raping came to an end. Grabbing his head, I whispered in his ear

'Do you like pain guard? Well...I can't hear you...Haha!'

As it was a lubricated area thanks to myself. I replaced my penis with his truncheon! See it would need lubricating as I am modest, my dick is no truncheon. A gay man would enjoy that as a dildo. Painful, it must have been as looking at his face whilst doing all this, he did not seem to take enjoyment. He was more occupied in trying to spit out the boxers, and crying as well. Such an ungrateful man!

Crack, straight across the back of my head. Not paying attention towards the door. The guards entered. I was trying to make a new friend!! Without reaction time from myself the multiple guards entered, hitting and swinging making sure I fell. Disabling any movement as the truncheon went straight across my neck.

34

Waking up, the pain through my neck was just unbearable with one eye sore. The song had stopped with it still being the day before. Oh no, throwing myself out of bed looking underneath for the hammer I possessed. It had gone as though it was never there. Falling to the back of the cell, knee's rising towards my head, wrapping my hands around them turning myself into a small retained package. You met the evil inside me? The alter ego I try so hard to hide. He did show himself to you, he would of presented himself as The Game. This is not good. It's through him that I am here, all his fault. What has he done now? This is not the previous cell I started this sentence in, what cell is this?

'Are you proud of yourself Danny?' the guard I mentioned earlier from the asylum was talking to me.

'Am I proud of what? What have I done guard?' turning my head at him as the questions. Whilst looking at me in disgust although anger would be the better emotion. The tension mounting from this guard was clearly not anger. Returning with questions to answer his just seemed to add fuel to the fire.

'You killed one of my closest friends as well as paralyzing another with the use of a sledge hammer. I have no idea how you got your grotty hands on that but at this moment it is far from the point. Killing one, raping two people. One through agony already put on him. You dare to ask?' breaking down with emotional tears, just walking off to prevent anymore injustice. Not quite what I had in mind. Through the lack of been careful, The Game took over. As another lifetime been a host to a greater power.

When the guard returned he repeated the previous question. Was I proud of my accomplishment? Not completely, the second was never meant to occur. However I could tell you, that ego of mine would be in utter bliss of the execution.

'No guard. You really have to believe me, it was not me.'

'Really? Who was it? The exorcist.'

'It was him, The Game...' The guard was far from amused in the slightest.

'WHAT THE FUCK IS THE GAME?' Shouting to make his point heard and understandable.

Without speaking, I gave an answer just by nodding my head. Now the guard just opened the door. Was there belief? No. He came to beat the life right out of me as an image to the way I beat his friend. The other guard on duty approached him with such speed to pull him off and back to the door. Once outside the second guard just told the guard to take his break and calm down. Regret was neither of the guard's choice of emotion as I lay beaten and bleeding. The guard performed his job, calmed the situation and made sure I was alive unfortunately.

Danny just told every guard he came across he did nothing wrong and certainly killed nobody. The alter ego has yet taken over since the incident. Trying my hardest not to fall asleep. In the corner of the cell whilst starting to rock singing rock a bye baby upon a continuous loop. Every guard was annoyed and more angry who all want to get their piece of me. Access to my cell was not permitted apart from the guards on duty approaching in two's if needed. Food was pushed in to the cell through the small window on the door. It was made clear to me that once eaten the tray had to be brought forward or suffer the consequences. But I have done nothing wrong. Why will nobody believe me? Rock a bye baby in the tree top just satisfied the alone time in which I was rewarded. Without purpose cradling just came naturally. Rocking back and forth. To secrete bodily fluids I needed the toilet, no Hilton hotel with en-suite bathroom. Movement besides the cradling just seemed out of reach. In that situation I sat without the energy to remove any clothes I urinate. This also allowed the rhythm of the song not to be lost.

The window opens.

'Food time, Danny, due to legal requirements unfortunately we have to feed you. Making sure we remain the better people by not breaking the law through murder.' just to show his feelings towards myself he thinks I don't see him spit right in my food. I really don't think he cares. They did not even ask how my stay is going or can anything be done to comfort me. Again I believe this to be rude. Not the best hotel around!

'You have got to eat Danny.' Still cradling and making the song louder. The outside world becoming further and further away. Allowing time to eat, a guard returned to get the tray. After seeing it had not moved or been touched.

The guard walked away to return with two more guards and a nurse. It did not bother me the amount of people in the cell. One guard grabbed upon by feet pulling as fast as he could. With the bouncing of my head against the wall whilst the other two pinned me down. This allowed the nurse to inject a serum into my neck. The room started to daze with my vision slowly disappearing making me fall into a deep sleep. Before I entered this coma my hearing was still intact.

'What the hell is that smell?' as one guard stated
'Nurse, I'm sorry, you're on your own' I imagine this one had covered his mouth and nose, preventing the smell to cause sickness.

The scenario running through my head as I envision it is one guard leaves the cell, leaving the guard and nurse with a final guard. A realization came to the guard that I was an enclosed human toilet releasing into my clothes when required. Admitting to myself when awake the smell did have an unbearable sent about it. Caring about such a small factor could disturb the rhythm of the song. I would not allow that to happen, it could not. What an achievement to think one of them was surely close to, if not sick.

Opening my eyes slowly but surely, the body feeling tight whilst fatigued. The worst thing about waking up came the headache from hell, just thinking I want to go back to sleep. Twisting the arms, moving the legs as far as physically possible in this situation. It would not happen, with straps retaining me to the bed. Ha! Strapped whilst been coated in a straight jacket. It bothered me still, what did I do? Should I ask again? Has some one not told me? Never mind, let's annoy someone.

'Hello, helloooo! Anybody there? I can see little green men! Is this normal?' the nurse walked in followed by a guard as routine states.

'Good morning Danny, Would you like your medicine now? To help the little green men go away.'

Medicine, a minute ago, I was in prison. Oh yeah, before I forget, Danny is my first name however nobody calls me that.

37

'Don't worry Danny, it was another episode. Little green men are not there, The Game isn't real. Ok.' personally I believe she was the insane one, yet it's me in the jacket and strapped to a bed.

'Nurse before you leave, what crime in prison did I commit to arrive here?' The guard grabs her arm dragging to the door.

'I'm telling you nurse, you better not tell him. I won't relive that all over again. The first time hurt enough.''

The nurse was more aggressive than how she may appear to the naked eye. Jerking the arm off the guard telling him.

'I am the Nurse. This is my department. I am the authority. You are here for my protection. I need to know why he does what he does. The psychological mind of this man needs to be discovered. If you can't accept that, just leave. OK.' staring straight at the guard making her point clear. Storming off without a reply, I think more embarrassed than anything.

'Daniel, please tell me do you remember what happened in prison? I think you're trying to wind people up. Are you?'

'Me? No never, would not dream of it. Please nurse, call me Danny. I'm a little embarrassed as well as slightly more offended by Daniel.'

'Ok, Danny. As you wish. You crippled a guard. That was not the worst of it. Has it come back to you as the prior event before that?'

'Really? Wow, what else? Sounds interesting.'

Through despair I received the final piece of this puzzle.

'Before crippling the guard, you killed another.'

Rage set in, throwing myself side to side.

'NO I DIDN'T, IT WASN'T ME' Tears rolling down my face with the start of a crying motion. The nurse replies.

'The Game, as you call him. He is NOT real, to put it simply Danny. He is just a figment of your imagination. Through my help we are

38

going to make him disappear.' Shaking my head as the nurse once again injects the so called medicine I needed.

Well friends, I hope you are my friends. This was a difficult journey as to how I got here in the mental institution. Now you have learnt who and what I'm capable of. The next stage of educating you is how I got to prison. In my mind a far more pleasant journey. An up and down experience in comparison to a rollercoaster even at speed. Speak to you in the morning. Night, night.

CHAPTER FIVE

Morning...Eight years old walking to school with at the time, my best friend. Introducing Euan. Lovely name is it not, African origin I believe. He is as you say, A half cast colour. With a black father and white mother. Euan lived in a really big house, almost mansion like. It was phenomenal. The door to the mansion was always closed. When speaking to Euan it was always at the door, nobody ever got invited in. In the morning, Euan met me at the gate. Then we walked the small road that led us towards school. It was a safe time, sexual predators known as paedophiles were rare, with the school being only a five minute walk.

Every day, Monday to Friday we walked the path whilst messing around starting the day with such joyful rhythm that was physically possible. At playtime we were there together, lunch as well. Three thirty came as the bell would ring allowing us the walk straight back home.

When I tuned nine years old, my parents decided to move to the area whilst setting up abode elsewhere. Eight years old I waved good bye to a best friend at the end of the school year. An unbearable task for a child at such an age to develop such emotional awareness along with over whelming senses that would usually be shown only towards our parents. The emotion required to do such that task, that was a truly painful endeavour.

We moved to an area that was more Muslim occupied. The local council covering their backs. This was a move to decrease violence with racial abuse if ethnic minority groups lived if as one. During this time, I went to a C of E primary school, Church of England as within the grounds of the school was St. Michael's church. Through this school the most important life lessons were taught.

I went to school every day as expected and defined by government law that children from seven to fifteen attended. There were only eight Christian people. A dark coloured lad who I imagine to be Christian as well. His name was Rocky. Very quickly he became my new best friend, allowing me to put the past of Euan behind me. The rest of the class appeared to be Muslim, however that is a vague statement based purely on colour. A Church of England school with more Muslims

40

than Christians with an average of thirty two people in a class.

Rocky was amazing. Every Sunday I would go round his house to play however in the morning including his dad we all sat to watch the Basketball. A good game at the time would be L.A Lakers vs. The Chicago Bull's. An uncompressed rivalry. Even to date the happiest time of my life. A life lesson was that racism through any group was unnecessary. No matter race, colour or creed we are all one race that are born with the ultimate end, that nothing can alter. To change my life once again a year later along came secondary school. Rocky chose and went to Harper green as I chose Little Lever.

A difficult change to life would be moving to secondary school. Once again meeting and making new friends. I had learned a new place. A lesson already to myself, did I really need to go through once again. Apparently so. Little Lever turned out not to be a bad place. Five years in this domain won't be that bad. Easily I could make new friends, now I'm not worried. First day all the first year's (Year seven as we were known to the teachers.) All gathered in the sports hall before anything could happen. In silence sitting looking at the head teacher. As far as teaching went this lady had paid her dues with the promotion to head just made her an overpaid, glorified pen pusher.

First of all the welcoming speech. Followed by the telling that we will all be put into forms. I sit there looking around at my fellow peers. A face stands out however if it's who I think it is then this school was a far distance for him to travel every day. Form two his name shouted, Euan along with his last name obviously in case another Euan was in the room. He stood to join the rest of his form so he would be taken to his form room.

Excitement rushing through the veins of a little eleven year old with the anticipation of the fact he already had a friend. Of course there were always the others who came from St. Michaels. So one way or another I would know somebody. A difference without offending those from the primary school. The value of mine and Euan's friendship. Primary school no matter my age I always excelled to be the top of the class through the mind. Just not smart enough to make the town grammar school. There was also the expense to attend the school just out of reach to my parents. To fit in amongst snobbish children looking down on every move I make. These children were raised by adults who had a town house and a holiday home with at least three cars. Not a problem the money to take the same exam five years later not making much sense to me.

The bell rang, signalling first break in which we had fifteen minutes to rest our minds. Through this time I went in search of Euan. I said

'Hello, it's me Danny from Lady Bridge.' He just looked at me without care. Out of politeness or routine he returned the gesture. Then he walked away.

Was I not good enough to remain his friend, or did he just not remember. Confusion just built, were them factors good enough to dispel anyone let alone, one who claimed to already know him. Clarity came to surface the situation two hours later. Intelligence played its part. I was always smarter than Euan, even at that age it was shown. Euan was placed one set above special needs class, although lucky for him he did not care. Even to this day the family would be there to allow him to fall and make any mistake of his choosing, he would be just picked back up to be sent on his merry way again. Intelligence placed me in set one, remaining in that environment all the way through secondary school. I should have looked down at him, as I am better no doubt not to be the other way round. Something did strike me as wrong. Every time he passed me in the corridor he did say 'hi' If time was available he would ask

'You, alrite?' In which in this town was a polite hello that you really did not need to reply just nod your head to accept the gesture. Strange I know.

Before we move any further let us go over a few things. Starting with my appearance for the first three years of school. Imagine the fifties comb over except without the gel to hold anything in place, was the hairstyle of choice. A side sweep. A dorky, geeky smile with a chubby body and at the time big trophy sized ears. The appearance along with the hair cut was not the foremost reason I stood out it turned out to be the over whelming height of an eleven year old. Standing just under six foot tall. Sexual conduct did not mean a thing to anyone until around the end of year ten, but the overall appearance that I cast amongst my peers did not make me popular towards the girls. The only people treated worse than myself were those in special needs. However there were two more victims. These were probably two of the smartest in our year called Darren and Richard. They became friends very quickly remaining that way throughout school. I could not imagine what went through their minds, what they felt or the emotional turmoil they suffered as nobody stuck up for them. Talk about isolation. Bullying had reached a new level which occurred to these two alone. As children without the morality, does this still allow us to continue? Constructive criticism can only make the target stronger. Remember sticks and stones.

As shown secondary school just did not have happy memories at the start. However it was year nine in front of the whole form a girl whose name I shall never forget, Mya. Unfortunately it turned out to be her last year as she moved away. Just as a bully would slowly approach me.

'Look at you, God when will change? You are just a geek. You have a fifties haircut with the fact nobody likes you, hahaha!' Making sure her point was made, to receive approval she then turned to her friends in the room laughing as though a hit man had done the job worthy of the price at hand.

Embarrassment did not end with not just her laughing now everyone joined in. Standing right before I could not reply as offensive the comments bought forward the motion I needed to cry. Thinking of that moment to this very day still brings a tear. If I ever came across Mya again I would like to thank her. Those despicable comments that summer changed my life. One week left of summer break, I changed hair dressers telling the stylists what I wanted from this visit.

'I would like that style please.' pointing towards the male stylist who had short spiky hair. Fashionable and liked amongst his peers if not others, it was plainly obvious. An enigma left his body this was clear. I want that when I enter a room. People to just stop and stare at what stood before them. Twenty minutes later I got it as I left the hairdressers. Before leaving I bought a product of the stylist, a holding gel allowing me to leave wanting to return. Change had occurred, evolution taking its place through growth of a child. Decades have passed since that style was in fashion, Now the change would start with me. Welcome the birth of The Game. Not present in my head yet, confidence rising at an Olympic speed.

CHAPTER SIX

First day back school bringing the joy that there was only two years remaining in this hell hole. A face with a smile upon it. A new hair style, accompanied by the booming confidence allowing myself to believe I was ready to take on the world. Bullying, you want to bully me? I suggest it's time to bring your A game. Walking into the form room it was made clear she had gone. Shame!! No great loss or expense.

Euan became the main reason as to my entrance to prison. It was through him, the experience that he introduced upon myself. The heel or enemy to the book. That table he taught as to where he introduced his knowledge became the birthplace and origin of The Game. One minute all this will be revealed to provide you with some structure and therefore make everything make sense.

During the summer of that year I gathered new friends bringing the bond of trust, loyalty even love amongst peers. Those friends remain to this very day. Always in my mind. It was this friendship that I was guided to decisions and meetings of girl's that were not just in school uniform. At an age of becoming a teenager showing the need of soon to be sexual desire. As any person would tell you, the more you talk to different people in different situations, confidence will surely build. Out of my control. Rejection would break the barrier of confidence within.

It was incredible feeling at the age of fifteen practicing oral sex learning more of female anatomy both inside and out. Time proven that sex could not be retained to any teenagers mind, the thing to think about. As mammals the orgasm provided to us allowing sex to be a pleasure not just the reason to multiply. Heat like the dog expressed itself to this fifteen year old. Shortly I had the honour of taking the virginity of an innocent girlfriend. It was great, painful for her as the insertion began soon to become insatiable for us both after a little time and practice. Pain was what she felt. I really didn't care as for that brief period the urge was fulfilled. A sick, sad speech that even at that age could it be humane that I guarded emotion, a dead heart maybe. Today as I lay talking to you it doesn't bring forward anything. The rest of school and even college women just simple elements of lust. Understand I can't be the only one to treat the opposite sex like a toy.

Before the age of twenty-thee the amount of women I had managed to sleep with was well into the twenties. This for some may not be very much however to myself I consider it to be an accomplishment. Over fifty percent of those women are nameless with an almost ghost like presence in my mind. At the time of question both achieved an evening of passion along with heated lust.

Ibiza was always the lad's holiday choosing. Through imagination alone just describes the situations we found ourselves in. One time I drank myself so stupidly it caused a reaction of consequence. An alcoholic seizure occurred almost identical to an epileptic seizure. Not through the day, not whilst drinking but strangely within my sleep. Why not just throw up in the toilet, like every other drunk person. Waking up in the middle of the night, seeing blood over the pillow with the presumption it could only be a nose bleed. Going to the bathroom to clean myself up, it woke Dale as he saw me walk towards the bathroom. Approaching my room asking if I was ok. Once at the bedroom, he looked down seeing pools of blood. Over the floor, the bed, the whole room just showed the signs of first degree murder. Dale ran waking the others describing to them I was covered in blood and needed a hospital. Everybody just crowded my space.

'Danny wake up, keep awake,' helping me get dressed, Dale and Sean accompanied me to the hospital. Leaving Paul and Chris to remain in the apartment to clean up. Finding the first thing in sight they used the white towels provided by the hotel from the bathroom. Could disaster only strike once like a lightning bolt? Wrong. As they cleaned, scrubbing to prevent stains the maid walked in ever so happy. As she stood looking down at the floor to envision two lads wiping up blood which lay all over the floor. Looking around the room she also saw any remaining blood spatter, yet to be cleaned. This lady screamed to the top of her lungs. Being a strict Catholic the maid just presumed these were sinners and murderers. With her English being at a minimal the event at hand was not to be sorted in the room. She ran in any direction that was not near our room. Paul went to reception to speak to the manager. All was sorted eventually without any arrests along with simple understanding from all involved.

However I was not so good. High on morphine, showing my beautiful smile at everybody who came within ten feet of me. My friends found this to be highly hilarious. During the night the seizure took control throwing me out of bed hitting my head on the bedside cabinet causing a cut straight across my eye. The collision was extremely powerful that it knocked me into a small coma status. Not to remember the event, I woke thinking it was nothing more than a nose bleed as that has happened once or twice. Over three days they preformed tests, brain scans whilst keeping me on a morphine drip. The honour was provided in the form of a visit from the British consulate. A private hospital I ended up in. In an overall opinion or to be cast as nothing more than a British thug who came to drink, party to cause a fight. Upon release finally, I was banned from alcohol which didn't matter as only two days were left remaining leaving myself to rehydrate by drinking bottles of water. Now I don't know if I was high on morphine still however confidence just reached a peak. I danced upon bars. Conversations started within anyone who would listen. The holiday not ruined just had a slight delay.

How does Euan fit into this part of your life? Euan was gone. I never wanted to see him again and if it happened it would have no meaning to me. Six months later, I purchased a gym at the age of twenty. Four floors which included an aerobics studio, a therapy room, Jacuzzi, steam room along with two saunas. The following six month proceeded. With my age came a lack of focus with the constant thought that tomorrow will always come. Things started to take a turn for the worst. I struggled to pay wages and pay the bills. Euan started to use the gym as a pay as you go member. One day he joked about buying the business. Thinking that a partner would improve the whole I had dug for myself. I asked Euan

'Ok, if you are serious about buying into it.'

'How much?' he asked

Looking around, thinking for a brief moment. 'Three grand, to invest in fifty percent of the business.'

Straight on the spot he agreed, shaking my hand then leaving the gym smiling. The next day he returned to the gym with his father. Saying his father would pay the money, whilst in his absence he ran it for him. His dad appointed a manager in Euan. Yet my money which he was meant to pay had not arrived with Euan presuming he had complete charge. I asked him, at what point do I meet your father again to get paid? It's still all my gym. The day after saw the arrival of his father.

46

'Hello Danny, remember me Mike, Euan's Father?' There stood an intimidating figure of a man. All the time keeping a straight face. Almost to the point I was just a game of poker he was playing. He told me about himself. Certain points were mentioned like he had owned a gym once before. By the Bolton council the building was deemed unsafe and had to be closed straight away. What a pile of bullshit this man spoke.

'When do I get paid?' Once again asking.

'Don't worry you will.' Mike returned later on in the week once again without payment. Let us talk Danny. That day brought forward the ice age of the business as I lost complete control. They just took over everything without paying a single penny to me. Stupidity brought the event that I was essentially robbed blind. Euan was smarter than first appeared, no good on paper, but knew how to get what he wanted. Mike was raising and teaching a potential conman.

CHAPTER SEVEN

The pitfall towards the hard life is an easy mistake if you don't follow the simple life. Euan or Mike never signed any piece of paper to show they were legally apart of the business. I was left to pick up all the pieces of failure. I was the one who had to face a panel of accountants to liquidize a limited company. It was I who had to face the magistrate to explain why the rent was never paid through my stay in the building, why the rates expected with the occupier were never paid. The total bill was forty six thousand to turn the key and open the doors. Without any consideration of every other presented question on a business plan. Financial success never started through this.

The council never provided a lease for the rent to be paid by myself or the limited company in which I owned, the leasehold still remained with the previous business. I appealed against the rates as not every floor or square foot was used. The efforts were useless. Father and son walked away without concern.

It was through Mike that every direct debit to pay out going bills was very quickly cancelled. Through this man, we only accepted cash as payment. He said it would make things a lot easier for all concerned. This was not true. He took the annual membership from two hundred to a mere ninety pounds. People paid, but how many people can you expect? The bait on the fishing line came to a very quick end. It all belonged to me and legally always did. It then got took down to seventy five pounds a year. Bargain! Or steal from the salesman.

The downfall accelerated faster and faster every minute. Before their arrival I had two hundred and fifty members at least of which seventy five percent paid monthly through direct debit. Literally they were robbing me blind. Luckily I was not that stupid.

The gym as stated was a limited company becoming an instant insurance policy when the council shut me down. For those who don't understand, in business you can be a sole trader and take everything personally. A limited company protects yourself from bankruptcy as the business will take the fall not you. The bank accounts, the wage slips, the assets. They all belong to the gym. As the director I signed a few pieces of paper to say the gym was unable to function. Then left it to the accountancy firm. Like sharks they took everything and sold the assets to pay the owing bills. All that remains is an empty, condemned building. Allowing me to simply walk away with a smile and peace of mind this young body was ready to party. All good things come to those when ready.

The business will always be a part of me. It taught me as I have previously said not to trust anyone. It taught me business ethics and morality required to succeed. Management skills came to me, as well as the knowledge the profits or till were not there to allow me to go to the local strip club. At the club till five am snorting cocaine. Buying bottles of Laurent and Perrier champagne at seventy five pound a bottle. Getting numerous strips making sure everything was removed. Great nights! The smell of sex along with dirty girls and cheap perfume. Pin stripe suits, a packet of old port cigars in my jacket pocket. No tie, an unbuttoned shirt. Leaving the family home on Saturday night only to return at sunrise Sunday morning.

I always left a minimum of two hundred pounds, in my wallet, my credit card and gym account card. Most nights I would go to the local hotel, their house or maybe the Jacuzzi if a girl was found to be good enough to fulfil my requirements.

Onetime I took two young girls back to the gym, downstairs into the Jacuzzi. High as a kite, pissed out of my head with two beautiful young girls up for anything. We stripped down to our underwear. One had a violet linen bra with matching knickers. The other was in dirty red silk and a skimpy little thong to match. Just imagine that for a second, I am! We took everything off. Starting to kiss each other, putting a threesome into motion. In a hot turned on bubbling Jacuzzi. The steam from the heat erected the passion further. It was brilliant watching two girls performing sexual tasks to each other so closely, then getting invited to enter the middle of them both. Showing fairness to both little ladies using the tongue towards one whilst placing the hands upon the other switching every brief moment. The only thing lacking amongst all three of us was condoms. Not to matter I'm sure the coke, booze and elements in the Jacuzzi such as chlorine would destroy any semen. The week after I went to the sexual clinic to get tested for any S.T.I (Sexually Transmitted Infection) Two girls that easy upon one meeting even struck fear into me.

I remember the day I took over the gym. Six am I arrived at the gym in a caramel suit, brown shoes, styled hair of course. Every morning this one member was present before the staff, Monday to Friday. A pleasant man however extremely annoying. Asking whilst getting out his car;

'Are you in court today or something?' laughing as though humour was the greatest part of his personality.

'Funny...I like that, Ha! NO I own this place.' That rapidly knocked the smile off his face.

'Good morning! In you go.' pointing through the doors to my new business. He walked by me, just gob smacked. I'm not even twenty five. Where did the money come from? That you don't need to know, it just happened to be the first of June. I even said when I woke 'White Rabbits.' I was told it would provide good luck if it was the first thing said on the first day of the month. An old wives tale? It did that day. Could you imagine people's expressions which included the staff? Everybody thought I was joking. I prefer sarcasm to jokes. This kind of humour requires a higher plain of intelligence to understand.

If only I had some sort of professional advice. Like a phoenix rising from the ashes it could have succeeded actually no, it would have. Pride as well been young but an end to that myth.

The gym was as important part of my life as from the age of sixteen I got into bodybuilding. Six days a week putting the human body through its ultimate pace close to breaking point. Two hours of training just pumped the adrenaline into every vein, artery even organ as anger was released through the simple sport. At the age of sixteen the build of mere thirteen stone by the age of twenty I stood a rippled Hercules at seventeen stone. True human image of universal perfection.

The Game became more important. It allowed me to push those barriers past the limits set upon by myself. Veins constantly pushing through to the surface of the skin. Like a tattoo these lines were a reminder of my hard work. A different take was the Game, not yet reached the status as shown in prison. The reason behind all this training was the need and wanting to compete in the under twenty ones Mr. Manchester Bodybuilding competition. Sixteen weeks of gruelling training. This included Thai boxing training, a personal trainer and a protein based diet format. Similar to the Atkins diet with just enough carbs to provide energy. I stunk all the time although it worked. The aim was to reach three percent body fat for the competition. I had a bright illuminated pink thong along with a spare ready to compete.

The human body isn't meant to feel or look like that. I did and how beautiful I looked. Third place was all I achieved in that competition. The judges had the mindset I was not perfect enough to win. My last year as a junior and all I reached was a mere third place. How it encourages me to jump for the ceiling. Who wants bronze? Third place does not prove you're a winner. Number one is what I am. I am the best in my eyes. Not this time, it was out of my control.

Upon reflection to get the body back to a healthy fifteen percent anything in front of me food wise was consumed. It was brilliant. I was allowed milk, biscuits, chocolate and even alcohol. Two days after the competition I felt recovered, so that evening I went out and got wasted. That competition only giving me bronze had built the grave and pushed my confidence into a casket ready to be put away for good.

The gym started to get into trouble. Confidence at the time was not required. Brains and an attitude that brought me to the dance in the first place. Of course then came the meeting of Euan. I could not function, it felt that I was close to breaking down. I thought Euan and dad were brought back to help me and solve the problem at hand. Clearly blinded by the illusion they brought to the dance.

The liquidation process in motion. The disappearance of father and son became the final straw causing the breakdown. The evil in the Game in which I had to pay for help and guidance to be provided. In all due fairness The Game when given a goal set out to get it without failure. Whether it was girls, money or to complete the training needed to make the human body perfect. Every time I had a seizure he gained control of the weak cell in which I am. He continued to possess the body until ready to rest.

However Euan and father had not realized who I had grown into. I was no longer a pathetic creature from school. I had brains, brawn and thanks to a bang on the head an alter ego.

What did they have? Nothing, the future will make sure of this. They walked around like they were something special, this was about to be sorted out. I would describe their lives as small time drug dealers. They dealt with small amounts of cocaine, the odd amount of cannabis and of course ringers. A ringer is not a drug, its stolen car with the number plates removed and the serial number to trace the vehicle scratched off. The same age as me Euan drove an R32 Volkswagen Golf. Lads our age would not get insured on such a vehicle. It would help if he had a license.

For years utter torment similar to the three years of school. Three weeks later they approached me walking a street. They had the nerve one time to approach me whilst going to the pub. They pulled over next to me in a two seater Porsche Boxster. Asking me for the money I apparently owed them. Telling me they wanted it next week or else. Where am I meant to get two grand from? Drug dealing or the sale of bad cars was not in my agenda. They can gladly get a return on their so called investment. I'm thinking body bags, the local morgue to end up in a casket far below finally covered from everyone. A guarantee I will provide after my thoughts they will need one of the options above. Question needed this plan in thinking that soon will be an execution. What am I talking about? People within this small town will soon come realize a power shift, if not a dictator has won an election!

CHAPTER EIGHT

The reasoning behind buying the gym was quite simple. It was quite simple as this would become the centre of my double life, a head office to my affairs in a private fashion. A drug dealer was stupid if not dangerous lifestyle for anyone to want. Death will show itself through many options in this trade. Every road chosen to take in life, drugs was highlighted upon its start almost with a tape of closure. Although a quick mention any drug needed even to this day could be made available through myself. Just ask. Anything you desire, if the price is applause able a deal shall be made.

Me and my little brother were due to start the invasion of this small town upon which we lived. The gym was the beginning. However through this greed became an element of the demise. Upon my side anyway.

Knowing the lads in the gym, the weekend was never short of the invitation to a night out. This at first was handy, getting to know what and where things lay. Research as such. To find out the price of a gram of coke, who provided it. The hardest and most feared man in the town along with simple things like that.

I tried my line first line of coke with a lad called John. He was skinny, tall although he did have an appearance about him. Without effort he managed to get girls just at the click of a finger. I in the mean time had to work my arse off just to approach them, let alone chat them up. Most times ending in complete utter failure. Until the champagne started flowing, allowing the gathering of their presence like flies round bottled beer. I did not complain that the essence that money was in me brought the night to pleasurable end. Whether it be hers or the floor at the back of the club, I fucked the brains out of them.

It worked though, the research I required on my behalf. At times just an expensive waste of time or night just the coke alone. A brilliant aid towards the night and all elements mentioned. After a while it just began to lose the edge it had at the start. Allowing my body to recover I quit it for a while.

The office at the gym was nearly prepared. Purely as the manager to this back street bodybuilding gym. The office would not suffice for what I had in mind over the up and coming years.

In the mean time my Brother was out with all his friends at the local pub. The handymen that associated themselves with him would play their part. One night an argument began with some little shit causing the whole lot of them gathered to be one.

'What the fuck are you looking at?' after watching their favourite football team lose.

A pissed up lad in the corner of the pub had the other teams shirt on, I believe the match was a local derby.

'Nowt, honest.' Was his reply barely unable to stand.

The lad was skinny, pale white face, puffy black eyes like this lad had another dependency. Looking like the signs of a small time heroin user. Either way the argument should not of started. It did unfold.

'You're still looking. Come here,' Shouting over to the useless pissed up man. Nobody told the two lads how to do anything, which is why they are so important to myself and future.

'Get your arse here.' they shouted once again

Without been able to stand properly and sight been so blurred, I refuse to believe he had any intention of offending the lads. He just managed to put his glass on the bar. Then managed to walk the direction towards the lads.

'Outside.Now.'

The characters in which we speak all went outside. As a murderer I can't figure the next part out. They were a key or element in my plans.

The both of them just began a beating or the start to an assassination of a weak disturbed little man. Kicking and punching, he just refused to fall or go down as it would end the beating. At one point he managed to push off both, just unable to walk way or run.

'What the fuck man. I don't owe you money. I am sure I don't urm I

54

Think anyway.'

To even touch, let alone try a physical assault amongst these two simpletons was offensive. One disappeared for a short period leaving the scene to only return with a chainsaw from the back of the works van. The other held the drunken pathetic to the floor. To proceed further to saw the hands and feet off during broad daylight.

Absolutely brilliant! Or even genius. Can you see why I needed such a beginning to an armada? Mafia bosses within the fifties were more discrete showing brains over brawn. Without payment to a deal set, brawn was required, if not used. Simplicity became my problem, as approaching two unforgiving scrotes to ask
    'Excuse me, you look rough, would you like a job as a hit man? If not, objects for you to just beat to a pulp.'

Would that go down well amongst any conversation? My brother introduced the two as associates in whom he trusted. Breaking the egg shell.

Theoretically I was the brains organizing the plan. Common sense along with a streetwise knowledge could be supplied through my brother. The place, business along with a financial investment all mine. Power requires an energy source.

The world around us an amazing size that with all the knowledge we know still undiscovered. A same basis to run an empire. A starting of previous experience. An element that with the right explosive set at the right temperature will provide an atom bomb in the making.

Ambition jumped upon a train journey leading further towards greed. A sensation blinded by passion began an unfortunate demise. A flaw that put a halt in the plan.

CHAPTER NINE

Opposite the house that the family of Euan occupied stood a cheap guest house. A main purpose of housing immigrants until they get every benefit possible and settled. No Hilton, cheap and cheerful, doing a job at hand. A shitty, grubby guest house serves a relevance to our story. Observation whilst stalking a victim, needed shelter.

First things first communication must be stopped. Cutting the phone wires, if a land line existed in the house now useless. Without a witness in site, the guest I return. Broadband or the internet didn't seem to be present. A house in the modern world without the must have technology. Bizarre! One job down, what next? An unregistered R32 must meet a fiery end, that once done, they could not report it. Shame though such a beautiful object.

Routine began as the next night roughly the same time, luck arose as the roads were empty. Aroma all over the air not to be broken. Taking a coat hanger and a screwdriver. I helped myself to a wanted piece of candy in the form of a car. Drove it towards the nearest park that was almost out of sight.

That was near Little Lever School, Known as Crompton Lodges Country Park. Drove carefully down the country dirt road stopping half way down between the lake and the road. Opened the petrol tank, placing a piece of fabric into the narrow tunnel. Stepping back still allowing room to place the naked flame too the fabric. A few seconds later, Bang! Leaving the floor as the explosion grew into a sheltered fireball disguising any part of a car. Exit time. A pleasant walk at a steady pace looking back, checking to see risings flames into the sky above. Part two now complete, bedtime.

That would have dented his ego, pissing him off. Trust allowed him to rob me blind. Punishment was far from over or even at a start point. Housing another two vehicles with each serving their own individual purposes. One car belonged to his mother whilst the final one to his grandfather. Punishment should not apply towards these two people. Relatives of our criminals was good enough reasoning for me. Blood thicker than water either way all must suffer. A hurdle to be jumped.

Day three was easy, the task of breaking the brake line on both vehicles. If they can't stop, they will eventually crash. Speed will be there end. A motorway pile is how I imagine it. Unfortunately the grandfather crashed first. It happened. The youngest died. The grandfather placed on life support through his accident putting him inches to death. The suffering mother mourning whilst guilt set in, out living her youngest with only a little scratch. A pain thinking they were a cause to death especially one of their own will be punishment better than death. Mourning a loved one, hard no matter an age, but a child will last all eternity. Not in my plan, close enough. Pain that personally I could not dish out, a force greater than me with a design of its own. Within the church grounds, out of sight I watched the small casket been buried with tears flooding the ground below as a plague almost. Why? Was a silent question been asked by everyone. Proud, I did not feel. Nothing to do with any part of this, to meet a final end without cause. Thinking a brief moment. Ok, thought about it. Fuck it! Mourning over. A blood tie, time would of brought to the game at hand. Granddad fell into resuscitation eventually the heart gave in, hearing the tone of flat line upon the machine. Staff showing emotion do that like to hear a sound showing death was out of their hands.

Television was a tool in a small degree with such programs as NCIS and most of all CSI. A program if broken down such as these enhanced the murder to be cleaner aiding the getaway. Showing what forensics will look for at a crime scene. Blood spatter once highlighted showing the position of the dead. The morgue through the autopsy process to provide cause of death. If you use a gun the element of GSR (Gun Shot residue.) The bullet would even help the solving of the case. A bullet would have an identity for example a nine mill has striated lines down the middle that upon firing get disturbed. Your gun will leave a signature almost recognizable to forensics.

What about a knife? Wrong, a weapon used in the outback of Australia to hunt with. It is prehistoric. Today's society makes possible the fact anything if used properly is a weapon. My prey is not a meal in wait. One or more victims to use the weapon on, not guaranteeing my life. Jackie Chan is not my name. It just makes the self defence easier leaving myself open to vulnerability. A young victim I am not going to be, especially to these two bastards.

My weapon of choosing is the sledge hammer. A beautiful admirable weapon as well tool. Dangerous at the use of a builder on site. One crack to the temple, The stomach and finally the back of the knee. Upon destruction of the victims you may disappear along with the weapon. Reasoning behind the choice is the slow painful death. The right hit at the temple with enough force increase brain damage.

Entrance to the house may be a consideration. Bang! Bang! The hammer just flew towards the door. Knocking back Euan's mother straight to the floor.

'Hi, debt collection, you ready to pay?' sarcastically smiling upon the mother with a hint of sadism in my eyes.

Crack towards Euan, Mike approaching the Scene with velocity improving the crack to his temple upon arrival. Unconscious they lay. Putting my focus completely towards the direction of the mother. Looking down, as slowly shaking off the collision, unsure as to what occurred. Money is owed, I want it back. For one second I turned to crack both father and son. Half an hour at least passed by before any movement out of them two.

Mother was a very attractive lady. A mid thirties lady who had provided this earth with children, still lay on the ground with perfectly large breasts. Why that matters, Well.

Her eyes lit up. Fear the expression expelled on her face. Hands reaching backwards, slowly pushing herself against the nearest wall. Her eyes circling the room, aiming her attention towards the phone, then the rest of the room. Finally I got her attention once again. Closer and closer I stepped until inches lay between us both.

'What do you want?..' Her lips shaking whilst asking

'Did I not just tell you? The conversation started that way surely. Unpaid debt which lies if the form of money, I am here to collect that which is owed by that beloved family of yours.'

'Money, What are you talking about? What money?'

'Money, Ok. Your husband and son, Owe me a lot of money, Once again. I can make this process a lot easier and quicker. Well you can! Saving any more hurt to occur than already received.'

'How? How can I help, what do you want so this can end?' Trembling still.

A pause dropped a silence between the two of us. One second that will provide the answer. Here it is.

'Drop your Knickers, get ready for the best fuck of your so called life. Otherwise somebody is going to die. That my little princess will not be me.' Her eyes lit up to think I am serious, is this real? Time was running out, to pace this up, I swung the toy once again at Euan and Mike. Keeping the both of them alive, just, allowing more time so I can have a little fun. She needed to make that decision otherwise next time luck will not prevail.

'Ok, ok.' Taking off her bra, and clothing then to finish her knickers.

Hard, rough fucking I gave her. Thinking of protection she started to dig her nails into me. Pleasing me further increasing the arousal within. Bored, I stopped half way through, just no passion or chemistry shown. Stood up, stepped back whilst fastening my pants. Pondering as to why I had stopped, she lay feeling used, broken and dirty. I had to stop before ejaculation. Reducing any D.N.A already within. Grabbing the hammer, looking thinking,

'Sorry, you had to go through this or get involved for that matter. Not your fault. However now you're a witness. I can't have that. Goodbye.' As previously described the hammer swung to end the life of an attractive young lady. In reality or the laws of physics it was not me that killed but mementum or gravity. I have no control on the forces that pulled that hammer down.

After that, I dragged Mike towards a chair in the corner of the room. In the kitchen I wondered to find a roll of silver tape. Strapping him to the chair restricting his movement, just leaving him with a small of amount of space to let him think he could escape to regain control. Waiting, watching allowing time to control us all until he came back to me. So did his son.

'Evening. All either one of you had to do. Pay me. It wouldn't of come to this. All your fault. Probably making a lot of people happy though.'

Mike finally opened his eyes to provide him with full vision, leaving Euan on the floor still too weak to get up. 'You have to watch this Mike. Sorry about your wife though. An accident really. Again suffering through you. Just to clear the air, with a little tweaking here and there maybe a good fuck. Just lay on the floor as I entered was just one way. A show you would have enjoyed, without doubt! The best erotic film you own would not beat the fucking show we provided.' Annoying Mike further, jerking trying to force freedom from the tape.

Kill number as he sat, the hammer swung right towards Euan's head. I'll describe this one. Like a game of golf, I'll be Tiger Woods. So the hammer in the same hold as the nine iron. You follow. Head at the bottom. Aimed for his eyes first followed by the mouth. Clearing room for the throat. Mike possessed enough strength through hatred to break free. Not realizing his son was most definitely dead or at least brain dead, useless in any account. Mike was turning out to be a formidable enemy. Control I had and he was not going to regain that. The hammer still gripped tightly in my hand. His knees instantly disabled as he ran within reaching distance. Downfall leading to this was lack of silence, as it was not wise to run screaming. Silence would of helped as I was distracted. Been crippled fortunately for him he fell back into the chair. In the meantime I made sure his son was dead.

Without choice Mike sat in the chair. Once dead, Mike crippled unable to function or defend himself. All he could do was watch as I continued his punishment. Euan now became the second raped person in the room. A star in a porno blessed with a live audience. You never know it may improve ratings. Screams were heard just leaving Mike's mouth. Lesson learned maybe. It may have finally sunk into the brain. You do not cross me, rip me off and least of all take me for ride ending in you threatening me.

'Death is now knocking on your door, Mike.'

Poetry in motion sank the hammer cracking the forehead. Entering the skull exposing a small hole towards the brain. I have seen a brain that close before. Nice. It upset me, as doing so in the murder he put blood on my hammer as access to brain occurred. Blood everywhere. The dam that was the head came crumbling bleeding out a river, almost a description of waterfall down his face. That really pissed me off, Stress began to build. What to do? Pick up the stained hammer and crack the chest cavity. A small of pleasure enough to release the stress just gained.

'Good bye, Buddy, Mike which ever. Game Over.' So I thought.

CHAPTER TEN

Over. The family all dead. The chapter of revenge closed. Admitting injuries happened without due cause however accidents happen. Their deaths were nothing more. I have influences that helped me plot and execute the plan. One person shone the light that was named the Yorkshire Ripper - Peter Sutcliffe. At Broad moor prison this man lives twenty five life sentences. A sentence brought to the man has his crimes included murder after which he sexually assaulted thirteen plus women between 1975 to 1982. Sanity has kept this man alive even though all he sees is confinement with certain restrictions and most of all no visitors. Although it does strike confusion as psychiatrists actually believe he is insane.

The Ripper had the belief he was agent of God providing the doings required. All his victims, he said were prostitutes and generally bad women. Deserving to die as sinners. Although some were just fourteen year old school girls. The Yorkshire Ripper clearly not a good man. Influence myself he did making himself a martyr encouraging if I don't like someone kill.

I never believed that I was doing God's work nor was I an agent of God. I do blame television as well for my actions. If it was not for television I would never have learnt how use a sledge hammer. Certain programs provided education as to committing the perfect murder. Thank you C.S.I all three series.

Childhood's brought dreams but most of all mainly nightmares. The fear causing sleepless nights to a point of refusing of going to bed in case the visions were true. Freddy Kruger, from the film 'Nightmare on Elm Street' My mum let me stay up late one night as fatigue was a long distance away. Instead of playing around making noise she said

'Would you like to watch this with mummy?'

Seemed like a good idea at the time, I did not know the difference between a horror film and a love film. With an ever growing belief that I was big and clever. I sat proud. I was not even ten years old when that film came out. My mother the provider of a tough love raising making me ready for life and the possible outcomes.

However intelligence was far greater to my mother. She knew the outcome of the film and the torture that would follow if I watched it with her. She was right. The plot of the story took a while to understand. Upon scary scenes arriving she made sure I watched them. After shouting

'You're old enough to stay up and watch it then you're going to watch it all. Otherwise it won't make any sense.'

Through total pretence I sat there looking like I enjoyed the sick, scary and nasty film. The encouraging statements that worse things may happen to little boys if I don't behave.

When the film finally ended, I stood gave my mum a kiss on the cheek and said good night. Like any other night of a small child quickly fell asleep. Standing over me he was. That stripy jumper through the film, the hat with them blades from the hand. Freddy Krugar was in my room, he come for this naughty boy. Sweat pouring out of me, I jumped up into sat up position and screamed ' He's here, Mummy! Freddy is here in my room.'

For almost six months the haunting continued completely out of my control. He was stronger than me, Freddy was a big man wanting me. He wouldn't go away, I had no way to get rid of him. At the end of the six months, my mother had enough forcing me to watch the film again. Without fear the second time, thinking he's done everything the same to the same people, he can't hurt me. If anything Mr. Krugar should fear me. Nightmare on Elm Street please, I put nightmares in your head. Fear of a creature of one's imagination is a silly concept. I bring reality to you. Freddy Krugar was not going to hurt me or you. If the world between the dead and reality allowed such a creature to exist he would need more than that hand to protect him from my capabilities. His face would be left until I persecuted the whole execution as revenge for the suffering I had to endure with lack of sleep.

Now when I watch a film I love it. It's so cheesy that the strings are almost visible in the film. However we must not forget that film is a classic and one of the best films ever produced.

Influence provided by a Dr Harold Shipman as well. What could be said about this man? He is just a freak. However the way he killed all those old people was pure genius. Getting away with his crime for so long makes me jealous. The wrong prescription, dosage or drug to finally make these over aged, waste of spaces disappear.

I lack the intelligence to create such an art. A prehistoric killing of barging into a confined space with just a sledge hammer. I feel like I have not fulfilled all my dreams. Don't get me wrong pleasure through testosterone satisfied me for a brief period. Hatred brought through vengeance caused the finishing of my victims. I feel like I could have continued to kill. The weapon been so large caused my eventual capture. Not completely sure how, thought I had that covered in the design structure.

The questions remains will be ever remembered in the history books as a great killer? I only kill the undeserved. They owed me money. The argument had to finish in what other way could it be settled? A treaty with both sides reaching a final agreement would make a lot more sense without consequence. Trust between both parties had reached breaking point. At weekends I imagine you not to tell your parents what mischief your companions and yourself were getting up in the age of been a teenager. Without doubt at some point the law in some way had being broken. Worse of all, due to punishment by the most feared respected in life. Was curfew ever broken?

A funny millennium as it progresses the crime in question is a rise and ongoing of paedophilia. It was rarely heard of as I was growing as a child. In the papers every other week a child is killed, sexually abused even raped. Every five minutes a child is taken in the United Kingdom alone. Some have sick minds to commit a criminally insane act. Some use the child as bate to gain payment for safe return, a mastermind act to blackmail parents. The lowest disrespectful of crimes even to any criminal a paedophile will endure more torture than humanly imaginable. However due to lack of control it wants out.

'Hello, once again! The Game remember.'

He does not half waffle on. The influences brought forward to allow the alter ego to kill. A self preaching, annoying, arrogant, Conesus and condescending little bastard. Yeah that's right I'm talking about my other half the weakling. Do you think if we ever married a young lady or he married a man, You can legally do that now in some countries. Would he explain he has a slight insane feature or just hide the insanity in a blanket?

Ok, If apparently I'm the alter ego. Why does Danny always, and truly I means preach that everybody has voice in creating an individual ego? Like fuck they do, I believe that all the coke, beer; champagne may have just pushed the boy over the cliff. No explanation needed, all them creating a black hole in the mechanical device of the brain.

There is no chance in hell that two of us exist it's not scientifically possible. Failure has fallen upon the shoulders upon reaching rock bottom in life, requiring something to talk too. When things are going well in this tale have you noticed I, The Game makes not a single appearance. A little biased and explanatory.

'Shut up..' Me, Danny again.

With a pint in hand getting ready to sing karaoke.. To warm the vocal cord I sing the loving ballad by Westlife

'Flying without Wings.'

A beautiful if not tearful song. What the states is far from real. Please don't believe him. The road is far from ending, with a lot more to tell you. Anyway my song, good evening, I'm going getting drunk. We all require some stress free time.

CHAPTER ELEVEN

When I killed my victims, Silence had to occur towards two people been my parents. Trust or lack of it would lead to hurt. From the minute of understanding the meaning of the word. My parents practically drilled the lyrics don't trust anyone. They don't trust you as they have their own agenda. Honesty the greatest moral yet a contradiction to trust. Trust would sometimes require a small lie. They may have introduced this glamorous creation to the world but once finding out the mischief I had been up to They quickly aided the putting me behind bars. That there is lack of justice reaching betrayal with the sharpest knife in the kitchen. I could not handle that. Well once finding out they double crossed me, before the action caught me. I proceeded to do the only thing I knew how to do in the situation at hand. Oh dear! I'll tell you now how that became an accomplishment.

'Wait one second there, Mr Game.. You can't just start going on massacres towards anyone who has had a bad stint with us. A release of anger , yes I agree but that what your doing could not be completed. The hatred your feeling could be put towards the uses of the army, volunteer to go to Iraq or something.'

'Now you have the cheek to butt in! Now you show your intentions and thoughts. You are all my fault in the first place as you need a shadow to face the truth. Upon creation, as I'm the one in control, Mr. Daniel Roberts, The Game will be played until the final whistle.

As a serial killer the design structure of any execution upon completion should happen close to previous examples. To be honest with you, the first family had the enjoyment of revenge and other killings won't have the same motivation. My family I will kill to shut their mouths. Proving their advice is not a metaphor but a literal meaning. So I would get away with the previous murders.

Should I use the hammer or change the weapon to strike my parents? For example I could fill the room with carbon monoxide causing the suffocation still with slow pain running towards the brain and heart. No, I could not allow that to happen. The time will vary between the deaths which may lead one to ring the services. The police would show arresting myself for attempted murder. The task performed by myself needs to be completed perfectly. In ten years when I'm been taught to children about the events of murder. The Game needs to look like an icon.

Separately they will die. Shift work is involved in father's job as a tram driver, so some days he could start work as early as five am whereas others he could finish as late as one am. Perfect time to think out the plan needed to kill this one. The mother has the draining, time consuming job has a long haul truck driver across Europe in mainly Italy as the final destination. Every six to eight weeks she returns for the weekend, so ample time to figure out the sequence in which she shall die.

First of all I allow them the present of seeing each other. Every relationship needs to rekindle the flame especially after such a time period apart. As a token of appreciation for a mere youth up bringing, their fare for the journey to hell will be first class. After one night together the onslaught shall begin.

Father had the unfortunate duty of an early shift. Perfect for myself, as for mother, well! Nine am crept up on the whole world. Killing one's mother with a sledge hammer showed the lack of respect. After all those hours in labour to bring me into this shit hole of a life existence. Creeping into the bedroom as silently as I could, picking up one of her husband's pillows, forcing it upon her face to remove all the oxygen. In a respectful manner she would not see the face of her killer. This would allow her to rest in peace. After three minutes of struggle to resist, her body just stopped. Showing no motion of movement. Task at hand was complete. A killing to be credited. A sick mind would cause such disgrace. I could not run the risk allowing her to open her mouth to anybody especially the police. She lay so restful, I wonder if the killing was a good thing as now she would not have to return to work. Early retirement!!! Next, the idea struck me, the following weekend was bonfire night. Hey, the costs of a funeral were a little out of reach especially for two funerals plus suspicion would be aroused, two been lay to rest from the same household without cause. The will would also be lost if caught for murder. I killed them so cheaply with the lesson to treat money with the respect and only buy what is needed, don't waste it. I'm not wasting it am I? To pay for the burial seemed a little out there. A wooden box, come on I could make my own then bury them in some vacant field. Cremation seemed the viable explanation and soon to be a free expense. Brilliant! Showing the true intelligence I possess in my mind.

'Excuse you. You can't do that... I will not allow it.'

Oh dear, the weasel is back. A creature we created should take its place and not be rude interrupting my time. I'll disappear when ready.

First things first, Father returned home. Not being the biological father I felt the sledge hammer would suit the ritual ahead. Cremated along with his long time beloved. Burnt allowing myself to watch them disintegrate. A beautiful kill it turned out to be. Executed like no other before him. As he walked through the back door after the long day at work. Bang. The hammer connected with the target, his temple, straight away. Knocking his head back, upon which it returned the hammer swung into the abdomen. Striking with such force that brought his arms across his stomach. Shouting the pain bringing the tears forward whilst falling to his knees. Agony was the only emotion running through this man. Standing beside the useless figure asking him.

'Are you happy? You should be, as now you will die joining the beloved within your heart. Yes wife has already reached the destination of death. I feel it's your turn. As the mourning process of such a passionate relationship could not fall up my shoulders. Sorry! No I'm not. Go to hell!'

His face just filled with disbelief with his eyes wide open realizing the situation at hand.

'Wait. You have killed my wife, No, You have killed your own mother?'

'Well, My friend it was you that taught me not to trust anyone and if that included my own mother, then well it's out of my control. You should be grateful for what I'm about to do. The odds of two people in a loving relationship, dying within hours of each other, then as a ritual ceremony you will be cremated. Those odds would be very high. The ritual I promise, similar to the times of Stone Henge. An anniversary present, yeah! How nice am I? Hahaha.'

A time consuming explanation later to provide fact of his approaching death. I continued to carry on swinging the hammer until no visualization was possible. Once again another victim lay dead before me, just lymph and numb.

In two days time they were about to be burned, well it was ok for guy forks to be burned alive upon the fifth of November. Fuel was needed to start and continue the fire. A local ware house nearby had some spare pallets always. I picked some up, placing them in the back yard of my new house. A petrol can of petrol to start the fire. Breaking some pallets to place in a mountain fashion, some flat underneath to place the body's. What a joyous occasion the fifth of November will turn out to be. Starting the fire, hiding the parents in a surely hidden position. As the Sunday quickly approached, I got the friends round for some beers and a bite to eat. Might as well make a night of it. You would go for a piss up after a funeral. No different here! A great night it turned out to be. I sincerely hope the friends enjoyed themselves.

'Just like that? You kill, cremate and celebrate. Bonfire night, what a celebration!'

Nowadays the nights begin to start a lot earlier. Amongst the days of November, the party began quite early roughly tea time. The petrol provided a second purpose covering the over powering scent coming from the bodies. Yet still no one knew the truth of the sacrificial lambs before them. I am genius, one hundred percent! As the flames reached the core of the pyramid providing a heat amongst the winter month we had this party. The back garden inducing the flames of Lucifer.

Marshmallows were melted on a stick to go with a lovely can of cold crisp cider. As well as the sweetness of sugar melted with a slight browning the bitterness of revenge made it's taste upon the sense. Alive they would be if they had the common sense to keep their stupid mouths shut. Fault of their own. Trust anyone lack of not a faraway concept. Life shall continue at my pace, my way under my rule. Children should not be raised in a cynical fashion as clearly shown I hate the world!

At the lovely age of twenty three . I already owned a cat. I thought the only creature that provided the true love and affection in which I desired. An empty love returned in favour as to which I fed her daily.

CHAPTER TWELVE

Depleted of money, confidence only more so present when I'm drunk. This also as an effect bringing forward an alter ego whenever it feels like making a scene. The ego within was getting stronger as the voice talking to me every second of everyday was slowly getting louder.

When eleven years old, living in the Great Lever area of the town. Friday night was absolutely brilliant as I would always go round to watch the greatest sport ever. Which turned out to be a well written soap or some nights a comedy, however still great entertainment known as wrestling. Entrance music to the superstar making their way towards the ring. Once in the ring access to a live microphone, to pretend to please the crowd or make the character be hated by the crowd. The funniest thing about this sport Is the fact they would spend up to twenty minutes in a ring beating the crap out of each other without creating a single bruise. Extraordinary!

That show brought forward the burning desire to have a muscular body that clearly stood out from an average person. I desired to have a physique of the gods. I wanted to be known as Chad Natural 'The Reflection of perfection' as no other man could even reach the perfect sculpture that I was made to be.

At secondary school I learnt that broad casting I watched wrestling as a timeless routine to be undisturbed, would far from make me many friends. With one exception to one of the friends that still remains to this very day. Thirteen, fourteen years of age I became friends with Chris.

That's not important, however the thing that made that situation funny was for two years we sat together in the form room, only to speak to each other when needed. Until that summer when I completely changed my hair style. Sean, who is now my best friend to this day, took me and a few others to house one night.

We started talking as though we had just really met. Yes, wrestling was the common denominator apart from the school. Having a favourite character made the conversations more interesting at dinner time.

Watching the sport was essential towards the birth of the Game or any alter ego talking to me. My life different have the glamour or any entrance music playing when entering a room filled with companions. Which, when I needed I sung myself.

'Fuck You!'

Here we go again, he is making up stories for you, how our creation came about. So now I'm leaving an actual live wrestling show. He could not win a body building contest, nor have the intelligence alone to run the gym as the managing director of a limited company. Yet through all that he actually believed that becoming a pro- wrestler was a potential career path. Please.

Lets iron a few things out. I'm the killer, I'm the anger within and only appear when absolutely essential. Right ok! I have a few things to say...

I need to find who is the ego performing the sexual ritual. I know it just randomly keeps popping into the story but where's the fun without it? A sexual encounter does require some turbulence or tension on the male part anyway. Otherwise it would literally be the missionary position. Which may be fine for the inexperienced such as the virgin or the lonely who are considering the encounter as lucky. As a continuing hobby to acquire women through lust. The same one position during sex is not going to please anyone. A simple workout with a little sweat showing and the release of an urge. Who decided that sex should be a spiritual act creating the bond of love? The binding of two people, to pass a soul to one another to become one forever.

'Fuck you. Oh and gladly read this as slow as possible, my middle finger.'

Danny a little upset with my belief on love making. Next thing on my mind, sports. A simple manly thing, as a woman doing house work! Reaching close to twenty four, I played hockey, rugby and finally athletics or at times Thai-boxing. Body building is the only sport in the world where one hundred percent had to be placed to receive the goal at hand.

I could not imagine my other half doing any of the sports mentioned. You get hurt, sometimes maybe dirty if lucky. Heaven forbid that

Danny got dirty. Looking at the hockey stick in my hand. The game of hockey is not soft nor is it a simple game. That's why girls play it more than men.. Why would I make a statement like that? It's true that women as a gender are smarter than the male species so the game of hockey is not primal enough for some.

The drug taking mentioned? Which part of the ego encouraged that then? I'll tell you something it was not me. That is a certain guarantee. It started with him during the summer, whilst turning fourteen. Starting to smoke pot, weed and hash. An encouragement I could not allow. He loved it , but I'll let him pleasure you with that story, give him something to do. Drugs take over the control needed to be in charge of the situation.

Music taste well… I like rap music or at times dependant on how I'm feeling that day maybe heavy rock. Danny the camp as purple that he is loves listening to cheesy music. The kind of music that causes laughter years after a split for example s club 7.

'Excuse me. What is wrong with taste for that kind of music?'

Hello again, Danny here. He's been hasn't he? It went black for a while plus time did not make any sense. So I would love to be a pro-wrestler. It will never happen. That you already know don't you? Any excuse to put me down always gets mentioned. It was me with the problem.

Yes, it's true I'm the one with the drink and occasional drug addiction dependent on where I am or who I'm with. Before I ended up in prison, I used to spend all day in the pub, go home for some tea then shower up to meet my friends later on that night, usually a Saturday night.

There was a complete time when I was with this girl. A period of the relationship of about six weeks there was never a day that went by where she did not see me sober. This was not a factor with her as it lasted for about a year.

One night whilst high off ecstasy I cheated on the girlfriend, and rang her in the process to show my achievement. We met for coffee the day after, for a moment she cried, but said ' We could get over this, the cheating could be forgotten.' I looked at her, then briefly told her it was over. Every day to this day I regret the decision to end it. Years later the thought was still in my mind along with the heart, eventually I got over

72

it, telling myself it was all my stupid fault, for the cause and demise. Time to move on from her.

At about the age of about fourteen, I had the pleasure of smoking my first joint. Liking the feeling expressed from such a little thing. It became a regular thing just in many forms. This included a joint of course, bongs and something else that I just can't remember at the present time. I never imagined things, it just made me smile and excited to the point I would hug random people. I bet the seventy's were a great period in time to be alive. Especially owning one of them Volkswagen camper vans.

One weekend I got all the friends round mine to watch the wrestling whilst having a bong or a magic circle. (Which is self explanatory really. Sit in a circle, pass the pipe with the cannabis in. Having your turn then, a brief moment to inhale providing you with the time of expression or point of view. Simple just blurt out the random shit you feel like saying.) Not really much in our naive lives to have an intellectual conversation at the best of times, as you could imagine the circle would have been an entertaining show.

At the time whilst watching the wrestling a character made his debut known as Edge. His entrance alone made him stand out as he appeared through the crowd with a gothic like appearance making sure nobody would know nothing about him. My friends could not understand why he was the favourite.

Through smoking the hazardous product of cannabis, my alter ego was created. The week after once back at school, just like Edge would do as a finishing move. I speared similar to a rugby tackle a friend straight to ground with a great amount of energy. Stood back up, looking down at him, started to sing to entrance music of Edge .

A month or so after another wrestler started to call himself The Game as he considered himself the cerebral assassin which make him the best in the business. Favouritism quickly switched to this man. So I started calling myself The Game as the arrogance and condescending view that I was above everyone. Why shouldn't I?

No harm was done to anyone. So it continued. I got a long term girlfriend who loved cheesy music so over a time of a close relationship I began to like this music genre. The wrestling thing and drug taking began to disintegrate through the severity of the relationship, as more time and attention went towards this young beauty.

Thinking I had got rid of wrestling thing inside of me, and now the detox making me completely drug free, no girlfriend either although we continued to have casual sex. I was nearly sixteen preparing to go to college so it was due happen once again. The meeting of new people with the difficulty of making new friends. What a joy!

I started to go with a more Gothic like appearance. Luckily enough still having my close friends by my side throughout the whole of college. I loved rock music, the girls were always the geeks from the school room but they were easy.

It was at this point that things took a turn for the worst. By the end of year I lost everything. No A level results due to alcohol abuse through a constant belief socializing came first. Did not take long for bad habits to return. No self- esteem, or confidence. What do I do now? Try rising from the ashes when only seeing a hole without a fire.

I took a sports therapy course. Gothic crowd were not welcome amongst this class. Slowly throughout the year doing the course the phase of being gothic came to its end. After that I started listening to rap music. Dressing in designer clothing. Desiring the best of everything. No need to settle for a copy when the original looks far better.

The sports therapy brought me confidence however nothing else. One spare night I started watching wrestling. Edge came out to face The Game. I really wanted Edge to win however the match ended in a draw.

Two wrestlers appeared through the crowd dressed as a Goths and one a vampire. They had arrived to protect Edge.

   'Again your babbling, this time about me. Yes your actually right that did occur. Now I'm taking over, bye Daniel.'

All that was true, however we joined a gym. The one that would eventually belong to something or body within this shell. A place where the education by others wanting the same goal as to look brilliant through the gaining of muscle mass. Every gym session he thought of wrestling whilst training, that's ok, it allowed myself the time to progress the intelligence that was already there with just a little dust. One night whilst getting drunk. I thought now was the right time to make presence known.

At a party in Mill's house was a lad who I liked to call Chip. Although due to the fact he had a chipped tooth. He had similar features almost to the point he looked like George Michael from the Wham! Days. He was at the party. A little drunk, maybe influenced by a little extra on the side, I just may have called him chip, unaware I had this name for him. He looked at me then threw the first punch.

'Now why does everybody hit or aim for the face?' Making sure everybody heard the statement that he had complete control.

Looking at me, a seventeen year old drunk and in utter disbelief after throwing his best punch. His opponent still stood right before his very eyes making sarcastic jokes. I had now taken over, I closed my fist, threw it straight at his mouth hoping to actually cause a breakage not just a half job chip. If the punch a full potential as desired I'll finish the job by a simple knee to the temple of a narrow minded subject. Paul pulled me off. It was over due to outside inference, being pulled away. Told to calm down whilst a beer came into my possession, reverting to Mr. Roberts. A creation had taken place that night that anyone was aware of, they just thought I had lost control. Well I've got to learn to walk before running, One thing at a time. Born I was but still weak as I did not hold complete control.

CHAPTER THIRTEEN

Waking up in which shortly after I would be released from isolation. Allowed back with the inmate's . They applauded my efforts, the guard on duty banging his truncheon against the wall.

'Shut it cockroaches...' Amused our guard was not.

Sitting amongst Rasta and associates, treating myself as royalty for killing a self righteous bully. Once the gratitude had set in, Rasta looked at me, however this time with an actual smile.

'Dude! You are really fucked up! Kinda glad I managed to get you that sledge hammer now.'

Shaking my hand. Now who is explaining this to you. Danny, or The Game? Well...

'Really you don't need to thank me for it. Just for the fact he bullied me and others, he called me names which does not well at any time. He most definitely deserved it. I well think so, hope so anyway. I did not kill anyone though, just squashed a cockroach as the guard would put it. No murder is never required, someone will always get hurt! ' Danny speaking in response to the ongoing card game.

Not understanding the situation on the inside of the brain. Laughter is all I received. They actually thought I was joking around with them to make all tension if any to disappear. It could not have been me, I have seen karate kid, I would not hurt a living creature. What has the creature done to physically hurt me?

The question now remains, inside for life, when will The Game re-appear? An ongoing thought if not fear. Respect from the people around me was a constant thing. Capabilities of myself quickly spread by word, whispers alone floating from mouth to mouth just for the internal committed crime alone. The crimes that brought one's self to this environment were never mentioned as no one gave a shit about them.

'3.11,3.12,3.13' just shouting these words for about five minutes

76

without no due cause.

Once again this brought forward the nurse, placing a sedative in my neck. Once again waking up in the mental institution ward within the prison walls. What sin has occurred now?

'Excuse me..somebody, anybody?' I shouted.

Without restraints this time just this room was different from last time as the padded cell was of different design. The padded cell could only really be described as a four wall mattress. Perfect little squares making up the room interior to prevent self harm or even suicide by the usual trying to bounce off the walls trying crack their heads or skulls.

What have I done now? Where is the Game? The nurse entered the cell been accompanied by the guard through protocol of purely protection. They held in front of me a small little cup with two pill's inside. No syringe this time. The guard even had my meal in his hand.

'Ok Danny, be a good boy, swallow these magical beans then Danny will allowed his dinner.'

In such a condescending fashion thinking that the medication actually be perceived as magical.

After swallowing the medication, the guard investigated my mouth to check they had been swallowed and not lay under the tongue. Upon acceptance that I had swallowed the pills, dinner was handed to me. A description of the so called meal is far from existence as I did not recognize it. Hunger took over causing the meal to be devoured as though I had not eaten in a while.

An hour or so later the guard returned, with a pair of chains. A set of handcuffs attached the chains creating restricted movement as previously used from the police station transportation to the prison. Must have mixed up prisoners as he really did not need to use them on me. Think this man has grudge against me for some reason, there was me thinking we were getting to know each other as the amount of time he comes to visit.

'No funny business, no trying to escape and most certainly you do not try to bum or rape me you dirty sick little bastard. Ok! Understood, course we are. Time for your therapy session. I personally believe you deserve the chair but no, what the fuck do I know? As you get the entitlement of therapy. Come on. People wonder why the economy and country are falling to pot. Trying to make these bastards sane for what reason. I'm the dumb fucking guard.'

Placing the chains upon me in preparation for my session. Then when ready, I was escorted to a similar room with a chair in this one with the therapist sat opposite. Of course my friend the guard stood in the corner keeping a caution Nate eye upon the proceedings. Through I.D coded doors and quite a lot may I mention. Just exactly how would I consider escape. Internal escape very unlikely then outside turns out to be even more impossible.

Taking a seat, coming face to face with an actual psychologist, however to make tensions reduced he preferred the term therapist. He also believed that without a condescending manner or intimidating factor of the word involving psycho. Sat opposite this man I had no idea for the actual purpose.

'3.13,3.13,3.13..' Just started to come blurting out of my mouth at the top of my voice. After a couple of minutes, I resumed a normal status as too the one I entered the room in.

'Are you ok?..I'm John your therapist. Do you know where you are?' Were those words coming out of his mouth, looking at me smiling. Suggesting yes I'm in here with you too but I go home every night.

Nodding my head, a twinkle in my eye. What is going on? Just random expressions along with shouting those numbers.

The first question out of John's mouth after the settlement period allowing myself to recover. He questioned the numbers. Placing a white board in front of me along with a marker placed in my hand.

'Right Danny, I would like you to write on the board in front of you everything your thinking about now, ok? I'll give you thirty minutes to do so. I truly believe that will be ample time.'

For thirty minutes uninterrupted all I could think or draw or liking 3.13 or 3.11 next to each other as though it was a random code. Nothing else, no families, no regret, absolutely nothing. John after the time ended, took the board away from me, along with the marker.

Analyzing the board only brought confusion to John however the passion to be re kindled. The following project at hand would be a true challenge. Maybe as a far out conclusion, the so called therapist would consider the code breaker to cure this brain. A strong willed naïve man. To be a prisoner the mind of the subject may be exactly the same in comparison to an average male. Therapy may not be required unless for himself.

It would not matter anyway if I was mentally insane due to the fact I'm in here for a life sentence, not going very far. The therapy for the problems that occurred whilst been in the cell. Curious as to what the people all over, actually think of me. I don't really help of any course as it has been made clear I will die in prison.

Back to the last fifteen minutes of the session. These numbers took over the session. The start of the end is a thought. They had a meaning to something in my life just I like most things I had no idea.

    'RED...3.13..RED..'

John called the nurse. He ordered instead of suggesting that the medication doubled. Making sure a needle sedative was given every night to put me to sleep. Concern rose upon the nurse's face, however she had no medical authority over this man's word.

    'Ok, sir I'll get that organized for tonight.' She replied

    'Good.' This time a straight face, no smile, no curiosity. Even after a session what knowledge had the man gained?

The medication served the purpose of providing a good night's sleep. Upon the serving of breakfast the guard looked at me as though I was a pitiful creature and this time they looked had lost its anger. What's going on I wonder. The guards as a single unit showed along with the feeling of hatred not pity. Like a drug user who took that one pill too many creating one stupid silly mistake.

After breakfast, medication was given as per usual. The prescription had been doubled both morning and night. Having a shower in complete isolation without any other cell mate. For the first time in prison I was all alone. The feeling of loneliness also besides as blissful. A repeat of every time I drank in a pub or bar throughout the week.

After the ten minutes, in the shower, I got dressed of course supervised. Shortly after, escorted to John. A daily occurrence it was turning out to be. Lucky maybe as people pay quite some money to talk shit to a person willing or look like their listening. Entering John's office, no longer the padded room as before. The white board present along with the page that was written from yesterday.

'Good morning Danny..How are you?' placing a sarcastic smile upon his face whilst asking the question.

Looking at him sideways, squinting whilst responding with a more sadistic smile. In doing so I took a seat to face the man with a direct eye level to read his thought through my answers.

'Well today, those numbers you wrote yesterday, you remember? I think that those need to be discovered with a meaning otherwise they will constantly haunt you. You don't want that now. That's today's session plan.'

No word response just the simplicity of a single nod to acknowledge the fact I am listening. Whilst contemplating what was he thinking just whilst he spoke his useless words of curing myself. This man known as John probably went to the best university or even better after graduating progressing further to do a post graduate degree. I stopped listening through the session, the same questions, the same talk over and over again becomes very tedious. Although one question did interrupt the thought process.

'Sorry, what was that?' I asked , to cover the tracks to suggest I was listening.

'What made you shout out all that over a two day period?' Was the question which so rudely interrupted me.

As I'm telling you, and then I told him

'I really have no idea as to the meaning of the numbers or the colour red. Is there any chance we could talk about something else, don't care

80

as to the subject maybe politics. Anything just to stop this over saturated subject.'

'What did you think of your mother?' John replied with

A stunning change of subject. Straight into my upraising along with memories I have of that. So random causing confusion that actually caught me off guard.

'Why do you ask? What have you got against my mother, you not like her? I think you should put that thought into a little pot and throw it right into the ocean, or nearest canal.'

'I clearly said no such thing, and sorry to say but your mother will be talked about regularly. You asked for the change of topic, so I politely adhered to your request. I believe you liked you mother and had no real reason to kill her or no so called desire within. The love towards your mother was never reflected in the same manner or attention for that matter. Throughout many years of doing this job, I am close.' John confidently spoke those words.

Change of subject true. At this point all I could do was laugh. Just trying to think of all those times that the feeling of love was expressed in an external manner. Love been the strongest word of the sentence. I really don't know, however John was the only person I was free to converse with at any time in this ward. Why not amuse all involved! Where is the harm?

'John I have no happy memories. Tough love is the method chose to raise me. Every day that passed I got taught and drilled into my head that the world is bad place and it is out to get you. Danny you will never win the war against the world. To get what you want you have to go and get it. Simple advice, the first rule that you doctor should follow. That is Don't Trust Anyone, D.T.A.'

John stopped writing for a minute looking at my expression the process of coming out with such an answer to a reasonable question. That smile quickly retracted and knocked off his mind numbing face. Eyes now strictly focused on my face, I imagine the best answer he has ever received, I would like to hope so. Placing his paper a side to take a sip of water from his paper cup. Thinking very carefully what to reply.

'Well…Danny I'm positive there was at least one time. Just once. I can tell you Danny that nobody is treated that bad, without any form of compassion from their own parents.'

'One?..Ok I may just have one, this one time we were on holiday. She took me and my brother to Cuba. My father could not come has all his holiday time at work had been used. Shame! Where was I..I know as a thank you one night, I bought my mother a shot of Hennessey which is almost similar to a fine Brandy but with a richer taste upon the tongue and lovely sensation once swallowed. Along with a Cuban cigar, drinking as though we were like the mafia or gangster's from the sixties. An incomparable night unlike any other.'

'Now, We are starting to get somewhere. Life was far from hard for you. Blaming anything that went wrong towards any life form which usually became your parents.' Thinking he cracked the case, a smile once again rose.

Anger rose through me, the surface of the skin becoming apparent in veins that were trying escape through my skin. Blood just surged through every passage. Providing an overdose of adrenaline. Maybe the therapist was close towards the answer if not right. Now was not the right time to finish this conversation.

'John I really suggest for your health that we change this subject until a further time. Your awaking The Game, or at least encouraging his presence. Please I feel uncomfortable. You have to do it. I would not like him to hurt you. Please just let me go back to my cell.'

Awaiting for John's response, my fists closed, muscles tensing, breathing slowing and becoming bigger breaths. It was due to happen shortly. The guard holding the top of his truncheon in preparation of any wrong doings. John for saw something, writing down on his pad his thoughts. Looking towards and nodding to suggest that the session had come to an end.

'Ok Danny, the session is now over, and the guard will take you back to your cell. We will talk again.'

Feeling a hand grip the top of the shoulder, the guard stood by my side looking down. No emotion expressed through this man, it was clear he was only doing the job to get the pay check. Escorted to the room door, taking a deep breath, turned my head and smiled at John in acceptance for the chat.

'Thank you, a well decided decision to end the session.'

The guard just dragged me out of the room, straight back to the cell.

CHAPTER FOURTEEN

I would like to mention this small factor before any murder took place. The following extension of the story explains how I signed, sealed my fate with the devil. I explained the birth of the ego and until this point he was a mere karaoke singer once drunk, a motivator to push the extrovert within to go get the female species. Now read the literature.

I love having an alter ego. Especially at the weekends mainly Friday nights. With having no money and little friends or company to join me on the evening out. I would take myself to the local pub to have a lovely cold crisp pint. Confidence was provided to do daft things including karaoke. I was actually booed! Off once. How embarrassing, a room full of nobodies getting up to make fools of themselves had the nerve to centre me out.

'Fucking one second here! You Danny, have been baffling all the way through this tale to broadcast I'm the bad one. When suited upon your happy self if anything goes wrong, I'm the one at fault. Admitting that you clearly depend upon me.'

'That is a little far stretched, not quite exactly what I had in mind throughout this explanation.' Talking to myself appearing strange to anybody within my presence.

A mirror was desperately needed. A mirror is what I require. Within minutes I was due to go into town for a hopeful good night out. A shower, yes to make myself clean for the approaching entertainment of others. A sterilization of the occurring day, getting rid of other's from me. Funnily enough it took the same amount of time to do my hair! As the shower, obviously figuratively speaking. A while was wasted in making sure it looked perfect. Every young man or women would do the same to impress even more on a weekend, in hope of finding a potential life partner. The night was not just an excuse to get popped up on drugs, wasted to the point of lack of stability due to the amount of alcohol induced in such a small period of time. However it usually ended up that way. Perfection was achieved to go out, drink and impress others.

'I'm still here, I want a word with you face to face.' Growing ever impatient The Game desperately wanted that conversation.

We are one unit, person, he is a figment of my imagination. I really do not want a conversation with him, or need to. Why? He is me. Yes I said it. I feel good, time is upon me to have fun and accomplish motives previously stated. Just as I reached the door, a eerie sensation fell straight through the whole of my returning back to the point of origin the brain. An unusual feeling I had never encountered.

The conversations were becoming louder as well as more public, at times a little too frequent. The insanity of an actual alter ego would automatically get a person sent to a nut house to achieve instant therapy as well as mind seeking to enquire how the ego came to surface. The last thing I needed was him to appear or be spoke of whilst I was drunk and enjoying myself for example: having the company of beautiful young brunette that I have been hopefully seeking. The craziness and embarrassment of talking to myself. I know I laugh and joke about seeing it occur in a public place. The young lady would definitely be lost for eternity.

After the sensation stopped I quickly returned to the bedroom. I stood in front of the large mirror hanging above the bed, a rectangular shape to show the body from waist up. Looking, if not staring or reaching to discover why I created the ego.

'Not arsed at this moment in time. I sincerely would like to know why half the time you claim I am the hatred and all the bad sustained in the brain. However then you claim I'm to do all your bidding requiring an outside the box confidence. Correct me if I'm wrong, a extroverted outgoing person wanting to socialize would be far happier than that of a self loving, scared to escape their own boundaries, introvert. Surely that in its self would certainly be a factor of great happiness and joy. Make your mind up, as to the need of this ego.'

'I don't really know, maybe it has some truth behind the statement. The ego always has things more correct than myself. Am I the bad person. Insanity is far from the impression I would like people to think of me.'

Still stood opposite the mirror, this time with a different motive. The outfit I wear along with my hair is now ready for the beginning of the night, so it shall start. The pub I ended up in on most occasions was the local which always had at least twenty people in who knew one another like a cloak and dagger society club. However these people knew me obviously, allowing myself free access to just relax bringing great joy.

'Right! Ok, explain this Danny.. You allowed these people or associates to rob you blind, you let them take control of a valuable asset that had true potential. The value held within that business, if you were not too damn stupid to acquire some sort of help. You just,'

deep breath

'You the stupid idiot that claims to be so smart, allowed them to walk away as though they were never involved or even in the building full stop. Now you have the nerve to want me to come out with you tonight, just to remain in a silent stasis. You. Yes you! Would still want myself the quiet ego to provide the ultimate confidence showing an outgoing, social able personality?'

The mirror, the reflection spoke to me as though I was having conversation with The Game.

'What was I meant to have done? What would have you the reader done in a different manner?'

I knew all along throughout speaking at the mirror the conversation was all one way, so I had to reply to nobody accept myself.

The conversation froze briefly . A one sided sadistic smile rose into the reflection shining back to my eyes. I have of things like this moment in time. I/we had watched many gangster films to achieve or acknowledge this very needed point. However to me, as Danny, It was all fiction just some films had been adapted from reality, some scenes had occurred through some sick mind. This just was not a green light for anyone to go out to copy or pay tribute to the original format.

The Game however believed to be a separate entity in himself with completely different opinions entirely of the subject and most things for that matter. There are role models as well as martyrs who deserve the pedestal in which they sit not those who try for complete control. Separate ideas through different identities provide a separate and much needed mind set.

86

' What would I have done? Just what would I have done? For a start I would not have let them get away with it. Showing the cracks through the scale of the business, providing the weakness of the victim before the attack. No justification has proven as to why they even came into the business idea, I would not of let it happen. Weakness is any man's downfall due to that first showing of fear.'

Well at I know that anger has a comfortable seat within my brain allowing the view of a good cinema. Although the expressions shown through the ego were becoming more apparent and increasingly towards the surface. What motive did he have, as well as his goal? He was most certainly pissed about something.

'It's time vengeance took its simple pace, you stupid little fucked dumb ass. Are you that stupid you can't see it?'

'Sorry, I'm now getting lost as to what you actually mean. How do we get vengeance and for what?' the reply I gave to that.

'Stupidity, is all that you are showing, somebody please slap him, you whatever, I'm not particularly bothered frankly!'

I just gazed once again pondering back towards the mirror losing all track of time or the night that should happen. Just processing the thought of vengeance. How would I get that upon those two thieving bastards? If it was a possible thing to accomplish what could be done to get it? Wonder if I could rely upon the uses of the ego, would it help if required? Time has come for the passing over to him to explain the rest.

Haha! There he goes yet again, If the going starts to get rough he slowly hides his fearing, stupid part straights towards a locked up cupboard. We are not a murderer. They conned him, in doing so they continued the hunt to take what they could in process robbing him blind. The deal he made with the mirror that Friday night.

'Weakness is all you express to carry out any substantial form of vengeance. Allow myself to take the role so I may fulfil it beyond the capabilities of yourself. Yes, Me The Game. Allow me to exist in complete human form and full control. After all the punishment that has been thrown at you by those two alone. Think of the outcome if I return the favour to them, in doing so make them pay the debt owed to yourself. Remembrance of the visit if allowed would be very partial if any, I promise you.'

'How long do you for see the actions you talk of to take? Really, you tell the truth when saying I will not remember a single thing? I take it the outcome as well as the design of the process need not be known?'

A simple reply that did not need any thought or time to accept the deal. How naïve of me.

'No, you have no need to show sign of worry, nobody is going to get hurt. The simple target to be achieved is to get back the lost/owed money along with the growing interest as if it was in the bank. Nothing more, nothing less. A sincere promise I will make straight to you, that I will possess the body as a host for a couple of weeks at the most.'

'Ok, I agree, yes. I take it the control begins straight away.'

There it was, I took over completely saving any time. Why wait till tomorrow when the task is right in front of one? Money became the thought after, initial plan. Anger drove a hole in every deem able place in the body, Pushing forward the signs of frustration. So I thought let's make a suitable name for myself instead of Danny. Horrible name.

I needed to plan out every last detail for this to work however costing valuable time unfortunately. After the transformation was complete I looked towards the mirror to see that the body was clearly dressed to go out. No need to waste the effort, would be a rude thing to do, and a sweet thank you to carry out his wish for the evening. I believe the time was roughly ten pm. One draw contained condoms, along with endearing collection of cigars including some very large hand rolled Cubans. Placing three into the palm of the hand, finding a lighter upon the bedside cabinet, along with four condoms. Better safe than sorry!! I would regret having some fucked up little whore finding me to say those horrible words,

'I'm pregnant.'

' Lovely, congratulations! Enjoy mother hood, hope you find the father soon!!' I'm not going to have anything like that, so I would give the girl that answer. Chose to head into town as it would provide a larger social scene than twenty nobodies.

88

The thought was still in the back of my mind to venture to the local pub. Fortunately the local in which he spoke, sat on the corner of the town centre. A stone's throw away from my final destination. I popped in to try to find a feeling that just was not available, I drank up then left. The atmosphere within the local was dreadful, if not driving a person to commit suicide, comforting I know. Shows the constant visits made by Danny. Suited him perfectly. Nothing to go after in a sexual, desirable way. No young women to prey on. Upon leaving, I gained a massive smile suggesting I had reason for coming to town on this Friday night. Time to find it.

I met a girl that night called Katy, I think. Don't quote me on that as there probably is a large possibility it was something else. A lovely, pleasant girl showing the signs that she was grown with morality. This turned out to be a negative thing as she was far from willing to put out on first appearances. I took her number then proceeded to pass mine onto her saying that I'll be in touch shortly.

A delay in going out on needless night with no profit from a waking up with a girl. Just wasted time causing an empty plane sheet of paper, with no plan or format. Involvement from any outside element was unnecessary, causing too much risk and the need of trust. I hire help, they find the subject, telling them that they are targets. A solo collection it will have to be.

With past and present luck of myself, I believe the use of a knife as a weapon would most likely end with me in the coffin! How could I make the debt transaction whilst making an image too the boat master in the underworld?

What could I do? Was murder an option including the mindset did I really want to kill them? Of course I did, silly questions. No doubt. The price had simply rose past the interest of the money to the price upon their heads. Running the gym created a constant running river of popularity. Every person who attended the gym, was likely to be of a different trade to the person opposite in the room. This meant I would know somebody for anything I needed. Still do to this very day.

Needing someone is an necessity that will always be desired if not required. The first price would have to be a small amount of trust to lay any deposit. The gym was a very small fish swimming in a large pond. Provision of certain amounts of respect also paid deposits if needed. So the task could be managed properly.

Of course I had to pay a visit to the top man in the gym to find out all the knowledge of Mike. The task at hand turned out to be quite difficult looking back. An outcome that was worth it and eternally rewarding.

Upon our meeting, it was far from what I was expecting. Showing up at a backstreet gym in a part of town known as Chorley. Full of bodybuilders built like houses with the completed chizzled, desirable body of perfection. Taken straight towards the manager's office upon arrival by two very large men, who were not too be messed with. Nothing glamorous about the meeting, even at the start or end a name wasn't given from his side of the conversation at hand. That inspired curiosity, however a time a place for that, so must stay focused to the work I already had laid before me.

I walked in to the office, all I heard was laughter coming from a man sat in a leather chair.

'Danny, Please take a seat' placing his hand out to direct me towards the chair at the opposite side of his desk to have a relaxed chat with a formal issue. As meetings that I have been to before the accommodating factor was comforting.

Once sat down and comfortable, the man looked at the escorts who brought me to the presence of this powering being. With that look or I would go as far as saying a scowl they disappeared. A great way to acknowledge power by nodding one's head to show complete satisfaction.

'Now, what can I get for you? as it is clearly obvious you've worked hard to gain time or even a handful of my busy schedule. Now tell me, what do you want?' Straight to the point looking at me briefly then raised his hand to read the time off his watch. A subtle hint for my response.

'Information?' Back straight, chin up as I gave the reply he so quickly desired from me.

'Haha! On what exactly? You've failed at running that shitty little gym!'

A very straight forward answer that was almost border line personal. He didn't care as the only thing he was thinking about was time, time which I was potentially wasting, which to any business man that meant money.

Billy was the name known to everyone within the gym was the gentleman I was speaking to. It does not take a genius to figure out that it was a persona to hide his actual identity. Roughly 6'4 in height and probably weighed an easy 16 stone if not more, nothing less. A clear injury was visible from the past which looked like a previous broken nose that had not healed in the original format. Perfect teeth, clean shaven. He sat back in the chair, in a well pressed black suit, white shirt and black tie. The look of an undertaker. A sign to come! Maybe as farfetched as sounds it just might have been fate. To symbolize this informer as an undertaker. The one doing both God's or Satan's work delivering the deserved.

'Mike Johnson and family. I also want to know what they do to make their money along with their placement in the pecking order as I have rough idea.'

Billy was far from amused showing through the pure facial expression given out. It was though I was joking or simply just showing disrespect for the mention of the name.

'Just exactly why would you need or want that sort of information?' Time became an issue forgotten, once that name or question was finished.

'Simple. They caused the downfall of my shitty little heap of a gym. Due to a very large tornado or allowing trust towards them. The gym was under a limited company so I accept the fact they were willing to become partners. Time just past, promises that the money to buy their half of the partnership would arrive tomorrow. It never came, they never signed any legal document to imply that they had anything to do with the business. Once they sucked the business dry, they packed up leaving me with any debts of the liquidation. I feel enough time has passed. Debt collection is an action in the frying pan. Retribution is needed. Any form or fashion will be sort after.'

'You want information, I'll get that, at a cost of course. I'll will even contribute by offering my services in collecting your debt. Are we agreed?'

Something was not quite right, just I was not a hundred percent certain. I wanted something, so the collection of my prize became one step closer.

'I'm in enough debt with the legal side of things. It all falls down to the price you demand.'

Given that as the reply, Proving I also could be straight forward to the gain an answer.

'I don't want your money. It's really simple. I'll help you in whatever you need to do with the information. After which you come and work for me as a right hand man. This way we will both get what we want, then you will gain more than me. Once working for me you will be taught how to do things properly. If you even think of screwing me over once accepting the terms of this agreement, you will end up like that gym of yours. Deceit is far from a gentleman's agreement. Death is basically the small print of the contract, if accepted of course. Would you like to take the contract?'

Again a striking stare with a thunderous impact suggesting he told the truth as well as the impact of fear upon his cliental.

I did not reply this time, just thought it over for a brief moment, that passed so quickly I'm sure it felt like a second. Without speaking the answer, it was traded through the same nod he gave his doormen. A contract excepted. I was not The Game through the meeting, it had the feeling of the Apprentice all through it. I imagine a character unmentioned at any point or just another unblocked alter ego. Time can only tell what it already has knowledge of.

CHAPTER FIFTEEN

The completion of contract with the devil has successfully occurred. However I feel that my original task is far from finished. Thankfully, this still leaves me in control of the weak and susceptible Danny. Let's get back to the story.

Sat one on one again with my soon to be my employer, Billy. A different day was upon us both at this second meeting with no actual physical change to his dress code of an undertaker. A uniform? Billy plays a large part in all of this. As previously stated, this is the beginning of a completely new game, I am nothing but an apprentice starting the life time training.

   'What have you got planned for them?' He asked as if I already knew, but truthfully the meetings we have had, are to gather intelligence upon a formidable enemy.

   'Not a clue!!' showing a childish smile of innocence, with the thought running through my mind suggesting to me that I was still in charge of something or the actual situation. Wrong, clearly I was wrong.

   'Have you ever killed anyone? Do you actually possess the knowledge of doing a simple task such as murder? I don't think you do, like what would you do if they fought back to take back control? They would kill you in self defence or ring the police. However the second unlikely as murder usually requires motive. They were a target for something or a connection to you somehow. If, God forbid you were actually caught, trailed and sent down for the crime of murder? How would you cope? Have you ever been inside? By just looking at you I am going to go out on a limb and say no. I also believe you would not survive in that environment.'

A true statement of a man who gets straight towards the point.

Clearly presenting the fact that knowledge equals power. It was showing that Billy was the fisherman of this pond for a simple and clear reason. Knowledge. However, how did he gain all of which he claims? He must know about in the way he talks about it in such an intensive manner. A formula kept in charge along with untouchable.

'Well Danny. I don't kill, it gets you into all kinds of trouble. Organization is my area of expertise allowing the cookie to crumble upon someone else if the worse was to happen. No repercussions.'

Just how did he get here. Looking around the office then at quick glance his face. It all fell into place, Billy was once a small time boxer. Explaining the nose.

Moving on. Mike Johnson. The information sort after. Now let's look at just who this family is. As they are not in this pecking order which suggest they are associated with the Manchester order. They would need the same power as Billy in a similar area to Billy to allowed or considered access to that meeting.

Billy knows them indeed as they tried to rip him off once. They tried with another gym to rip him off with money, gambling and cars. However Billy wanted to see what they would do next. That sequence of events turned out to fall upon my luck, with my shit heap of a gym.

Fifteen years ago a Mike Johnson was heard to have fled Stockport in the underground due to the fact of his eight year old son. Yes it's true, coincidently similar moving as my mother. Just I imagine different reasons. Mike came to Bolton allowing the feelings towards his family , control him and provide a definite crack showing the weakness. Never would Mike like any loving parent put their children or loved one's in business or choose work. It's one or the other in most cases.

Leaving a couple of years to allow settlement. A stable environment was formed to raise his son along with his beloved wife. Mike had secrets like us all, it's a human mistake. Mike owed a substantial amount of money in the Stockport region going under the name of Ryan Johnson at first. Then in the whirlwind of his demise in the town, the name changed to Mike.

At that time heroin was making a large comeback upon the social scene as it was so welcomed in the seventies. He was a small time dealer who thought progression came with rapid fire.

A small time dealer does not rapidly go from bottom to top of the ladder, same as a proper job. Buying in bulk hoping to get it cheap he started to lose custom. Reaching the point he kept on buying but not successful enough to sell it all. It was the business world as sales slow you cut the losses before buying your next order. Stupidly he did not. Now starting to receive threats off his suppliers. He banked up the cash. Bought a new identity then slid out of town, A worm will leave a trail!! He is still wanted for that money owed. Payment in any form would be suited to the suppliers. I imagine cash would actually come with interest on top of that. A new career was very clearly needed by this man. Mike was not going to give up on a life style to go work nine to five Monday to Friday. The justification in all that is he did not become a millionaire. Oh dear! The tears weep for his loss!

Without thinking Mike tried the cocaine market as a dealer for that area. Again not the smartest of ideas, an average person does account for his mistakes to progress further. Cocaine just over twelve years ago was far from the cheapest drug on the market. Therefore suppliers were very cautious as to who they sold the product to. The dealer approaching a supplier required a small amount of trust, the honour amongst thieves code. Suppliers had to watch that dealers were tagged, watched followed to the drop off point.

Euan was getting older. Mike started to finally think, to show his son to grow up with some morality. He kept the drug marketing to a minimal. Getting hold of a small business to run, bought a body shop, which included the services of two mechanics in the sale. The body shop turned out be a profitable business as it came with a small piece of land out front large enough to be turned into a car lot. Now along with a repair shop a local small time car sales man.

Providing a forefront the mechanics alone were bringing in enough income to show a decent profit margin. Cars started arriving fast to fill out the forecourt. Mike had actually created a small official business. Showing profits with two different parts to the element under the one roof and business. However Mike Johnson does not appear on the national register. Not because he never voted, that's not the issue. The way Mike Johnson changed his name was far from official. Probably paid for some dead guys details.

Welcome back Billy. Yes, Billy was running this town back then. Mike explained the situation in which he had got himself into. In doing so he insisted a George Myers was not to know. Billy got offended at been told what to do especially by this failure of a dealer.

' Yeah, Ok. I'll get your documents. Making everything official, The price is twenty grand. Quite reasonable I think for the product. That's not a debateable fee.' A man clearly in control with the demand and supply and of course pricing.

'You what?'

Mike getting a little wounded, Not the smallest fee, not the easiest product though. Mike stepped forward towards Billy causing four men to step forward as well, right beside him. Billy looked around then at his customer showing complete control along with gratitude of the sale.

'Did you honestly believe that you would be of any concern to me.. When that day arises, if it ever does, I'll gladly let you know. When you wake from it.'

With a constant smile through the conversation, the four men stood alongside Billy just laughing at Mike.

'Ok, I'll get you the money. Next week. You bring the documents back here to me.' Then Mike flew out of the room back to his car.

'He screws around with us in any sense of the word, you guys know what to do.'

As he walked away back towards his car. The four men stood as statues with a smile showing grace and gratitude. This due with that they would be allowed to hurt someone in a short space of time. If Mike failed in his end of the deal.

A week later in the same place the meeting occurs once again. Billy asks for the money, whilst Mike stands before Billy in desperation of the envelope containing the official new life of Mike Johnson. Through anxiety he passes a parcel over towards Billy in hope he won't get ripped off. The four men stood all in black including black leather gloves. Proudly in stance waiting that order to progress in a severe beating.

'Ok. Fair enough. However I will mention this on free terms Mike, Ryan whatever you want to be fucking called. This is my town, if you mess around with drugs, cars, anything really without my permission, I and my friends here will hunt you down and kill you. In a slow painful way, then the last thing you see, will be my face. Clear.'

Just walking off with his protectors, leaving little old Mike stood there contemplating his worthless future.

A few years passed without any mention about the family or our friend Mike. Except in the mid nineties it was a fashionable thing to invest or own a gymnasium. It became a fashionable hobby to attend a gym whether you needed too, or just for pretentious reasons.

Guess what? Mike picked up on this and in doing so, decided to set up a pay as you go gym, making a membership thing left to the bigger corporate companies. Oh dear. In all the money he was making he forgot the element of permission off a certain supplier. Mike continued the gym until close towards the new millennium. Decreasing the membership and fees over all caused the gym to maximise the safe zone in the amount of people in the fire safety and health regulations. The cheapness brought everybody in, it just could not accommodate.

After that gym actually shut down due to apparently, it failed building standards testing. Again a complete disappearance of Mike Johnson along with a lump sum of profit in actual cash, untraceable actually. That was the real reason as to the pay as you go scheme. Still he had yet to speak to Billy about the actual business from start to finish.

In the mean time Euan became of age, through laziness had no actual desire to work. The ringers industry started to arrive or pick upon the underworld. The selling of cars and hiring top end cars for the day was still a popular choice for father and now son. The son of course was now been prepared and inducted as such towards the takeover in the future.

All that time father or son had kept that close of a relationship even though they lived under the same roof. Not the most talkative family. Yet Euan was going round town on Fridays, Saturdays for nights out claiming he had become the top dog!

There is the information on father and son. Billy in 2006 got hold of the information about Mike and paid him a little visit.

'Hello Mike, Now the last time we encountered each other's

company. I politely told you something as a small part of our deal or contract. Did I not? Do you remember?'

With a shock of disbelief, along with horror Mike just before Billy. The entourage of course stood by his side. The meeting was less formal in the fact it happened outside the house. It looked rather stupid with them stood at the door way. They simply walked past Mike making themselves comfortable inside the house as though it was their own.

'Mike, I was a major factor in helping you create a legal identity. I would say through me helping you that way, it may sound far fetched now but I aided the fact you have this lovely home. Those documents helped your family, keeping them safe. How do you go about paying me back? Well...?'

Billy was far from amused at this point.

'Billy the gym thing was completely legal, I thought with it not effecting you or committing a criminal act, there was no need to inform you. Therefore I've done nothing wrong.'

Standing tall and proud in front of Billy providing an impression that he was most definitely the king of this castle.

'A criminal, You see me as criminal? You may be right, any way moving on. Business is still business. It was a making money business. I am sure I made it clear, no I guarantee I emphasized upon the issue I am the tax man in this town. When our deal was made I told you, cars, drugs or anything, I want you to ask for permission. You did not. Did you?.' His eyes glancing around the room of Mikes home.

'How much?' looking in disgust.

'Five, yeah after taxes and interest over the period of time the gym ran, Five grand.' Billy quoted.

Mike left the room still in the vision of the entourage. He returned with the sum of five thousand pounds all in twenties. Passing over to Billy who still sat comfortably upon the couch. Looking at the package, flicking through the notes. He then turned his attention back towards Mike as though all was settled and it was done and dusted. Then holding his arm in the air returned back to the original stance directly in front of Mike.

'I must mention before I forget. Your son is becoming a royal pain in the arse. Going around town at night telling people he is the top dog! Pissing in my yard and making a fool of me. This problem better be sorted out sooner rather than later is what I think. You better sort him...Good night!'

Mike told Euan about running his mouth, and that digression was of the up most importance in such a career path. However Euan was a young lad, did not listen to the advice been given. Went out that very weekend thinking and believing that his dad was just messing around with him, thinking it was a joke. Euan continued to run his mouth at every available opportunity.

The following Tuesday, Euan got pulled by a local police car. This then drove to a local car park at the far end of town away from any crowded area. This was the first time he had been formally introduced to Billy including associates.

'So Euan your now in charge...Really? Well son I'm taking over!!'

One punch from Billy's boxing days and training instantly threw Euan towards the other end of the car park. After the doing the deed, the four men threw themselves upon Euan like vultures picking at the pieces. Beating the holy hell out of the mouthy young lad.

'Make sure you leave enough of him, to send the message to his dad as apparently neither one pays attention in class.'

The cop that brought the subject to the park packed him into the backseat of the car. Kindly took him back to point of origin. Helped the boy get out of the police car and gladly placed him in the front seat of the car he got pulled in. A friendly police officer has he even told him to drive safe.

The message was sent thanks to Billy without any interference or showing up in the picture. The killing or planning will be a great and joyful thing to take part in. The lesson of how to prepare and kill will now be taught.

CHAPTER SIXTEEN

Remaining in the mental institution of the prison, another morning swiftly approached. Shortly after breakfast it was the usual visit to John my ever so friendly therapist. The same time, obviously the same place, I've kept my medicine this regular.

However the constant repeat of the previous conversation so this man could either break myself or the mythological code. My overall personality issue or figuring out this alter ego thing just kept been cast aside until that idea was cracked and filed. From a previous encounter, John quickly discovered that it was best not to bring up the mother topic just quite in the early stages.

John showed desperation in trying to figure out the rise of The Game at the same time. Hoping that within the approaching sessions he would finally meet him, without been physically threatened or at harm. This session I was bored so I simply sat staring at him, just like a cat playing with a mouse! Of course in such a pleasant environment that was not a cell. I had to smile as satisfaction was brought to me moving from one square room to another.

'Is that you Danny or do I get to talk to The Game? Who am I talking to?'

The questions first asked by John. Turning my head sideways I figured the silence on my behalf had to be broken.

'Without sounding rude John, do you honestly believe you would still be sat there in that chair continuing this mind exploration? If I allow The Game to be present.. I think the last time he nearly appeared you were offending my mother. Memories I'm sure not forgotten.'

'I was not trying to offend. I'm going to change the subject now. Would that be ok with yourself?' Tension or even harm was not John's prerogative.

'What would you like to know this time? As the choice of subject, you have already made your mind up.'

'Why do you two people rape both men as well as women? Including the act of necrophilia?'

'One thing I will tell you John as a lead, I like you. Rape as you already know is not all about sex. It's about over powering to show ultimate control. Now add that towards my case.'

Having to think about the questions presented to me in this session. I believed it was time of subject change for everyone's best interests. The question's were once again borderline personal. What was the need for those particular questions? Should I have answered them I wonder. This would most definitely leave me venerable. Allowing a passage to be created for John to enter my mind freely.

Oh well might as well answer. I have nothing else better to be getting on with for the rest of my life!!! See I still show sarcasm to you. I make a good host. Anyway focus, the questions.

'Rape? I would not call it rape. That's a very severe statement to make, even for yourself.'

'Ok, What would you call it when you as a person has performed a sexual act upon another human being without consent?'

John displeased with my answer as the tone became more aggressive than previously.

'Deserving...yeah I think that's what I would call it. All those people I got accused and trialled for. The people I so called performed sexual acts on without consent. I call them lucky or even blessed to be touched by me in such loving manner.'

Long pause which lasted roughly one minute.

'Hello John the therapist. You enquired about meeting me.' Smiling as John with the impression that we were the last two people on earth.

'What you're The Game now?' His tone gentle followed by a swallow of fear.

'Definitely...could you believe that other thing would glamour you with conversations such as that? The reason I took advantage of the situation was quite simple..'

A pause allowing John to think everything over.

'Well, what is it?' Showing anxiety with his response to the question.

'Do you really want to know? Well, I could. I wanted to. Hahaha! Yeah there is clearly no other reason . Women, men, just yeah. The time felt right for me. I was horny, seizing the moment as well as the fact nobody could answer back to the ultimate power I had over them.'

John was far from amused with the answer. Almost crying. Whatever The Game said had definitely touched a nerve.

'My daughter was nearly raped a few years ago. By men with the same similarity as you show and it was all because they had no power over anything and just because they wanted too. You treated those people like a child with toys. Once boredom set in, you cast it aside.'

Throwing his clip board down straight to the ground, leaping towards me showing an immense feeling of anger that even I could not express. However ruining the fun, the guard stepped in before anything actually happened. Kind of a shame really. I really hope he is not offended and that we get to meet tomorrow. I did not get chance to answer the whole question. Why do I rape dead people?

Luck that week was on my side which was an overdue issue. I got to see the following day or session, whichever. Returning to the session as Danny. There he stood not so proud at one side of the room, accompanied by two guards at either side of John. Not sure of the previous actions in the last session. It must have been in my favour, whatever it was.

'I warned you John, on numerous occasions and meeting yet you choose not to listen. You continue to try to access that personality. I am sorry for anything that happened in the previous session.'

'It's ok, this time I was at fault.' Pride clearly broken, now been swallowed all because a criminal took advantage of the open window. Cracking his personality accompanied by any hidden issues. Who could be perceived as the smarter element in that single session? Ironic!!

The session started after all apologies. It was all about the numbers. Once again the white board stood before us both still covered in ink since it was drawn upon. 3.13 covered the page in as many angles that the page would fit. The whole session was about where and what the meaning of the abnormality through the random numbers. Was it due a Bible reference, A possible chapter three, verse thirteen. Hardly, I would not say I am the most religious of people. At the end of the session, whilst standing in the chains around my wrist flew into the air as I screamed out those very numbers. Whilst unaware of the surrounding environment or anything going on inside it. Chains, flying in every possible direction that the restraints allowed. 3.13, red, 3.13.3131.3.313.313...red...no white. The chains continued to get in the way, so until I stopped I was just left shouting, screaming. John showing a slight fear long with sympathy I think, grabbed his clipboard to make notes, making sure the guards did not get involved.

One guard stepped back, radioing for the nurse to get to the room immediately. But like every other person in that room, she was nothing more than a useless tool. Finally the pandemonium came to an end. Nobody hurt, or offended this time. Quickly escorted back to my peaceful cell, once again injected with a sedative. I may become a walking bottle of the medicine shortly!! Either way I promptly went to sleep.

I tell you that the death penalty would have been far easier than this constant torture of needles, sedatives, medication and beatings off the guards when unsupervised.

Would it of been too easy for that judge to punish me with the sentence of death? One less convict costing taxes within the British prisons. One less convict to roam the world if ever released. A confusing error over cast through my brain as why they allowed me to live after all I had done.

Returning to the session, John had a tape player or something that allowed music to be played. He told me that he had a gift for me and the co-operation I had provided on the course. However I was not allowed to take it back to my cell.

'Why have you brought me a gift? What is it you want?' in a tone of anger or amusement which ever, it was not clear enough to be figured out.

'I have come ready and prepared to talk with The Game. The gift is his music theme tune. As you told me the other week. I looked for the song by Head Motor, thinking of you, I brought the song to the session.' John greatly pleased with himself.

'You really don't want to do whatever your planning next.' I just sat with patience waiting for him to press play.

I did not wait long. The song started. It was great, the guitars, the drums. The actual tone and pitch of the lead singer who sounded just like a pure rock God as well as legend.

We both sat there looking at each other. I even started singing along, swaying to the rhythm of the song. Nothing happened.

'This is the right song, now where is he? I have questions for him, bring him out or whatever it is you do to create it.'

The song played on a loop continuously for a whole hour. No progress made by myself or John. He was simply disgusted at the outcome of the session, a whole hour wasted. I think at this point John may have just realized that I have no control over The Game or the existed ego we talk of. I maybe sane like the average person. The little voice at the back of my head had no reason to present himself on this occasion, just because a song played.

My return to the comfortable cell in which I was accommodated. I lay looking at the ceiling above. Imagining at that specific moment, how the sky outside was painted or how the stars would shine that night following the day. Hopefully one day, or some other lifetime I would view the wonderful glow of Orion's Belt once again, The formation of three stars in a straight line. It was absolutely gorgeous. The whole consolation that formed Orion was indescribable to a man in confinement. It was the only thing I thought about, that truly got processed every time.

I had the best night's sleep I had in a long time obviously due to the medication however just without an extra sedative added to the equation. Upon waking up it actually occurred to me that I would have to see John at some point today. Yesterday he tried so hard to bring out

The Game. I thought about trying to convince him to release himself for the up and coming session without causing any harm towards John. Could it be done?

Sat down opposite the therapist. He said his welcome as normal, with a smile showing some form of regret. Holding back his actual thought process as every attempt had back lashed causing more problems towards him and not the patient. Circles at this point is the only direction we were moving in.

'Hello John. I believed I've been summoned upon yet again. How may I be of help today? I hope your daughter recovered from her ordeal.'

A look of hatred headed in my direction, only this time keeping his cool, been completely professional.

' Oh John I advise you try not to attack me today. As a hobby I would gladly rip off your face, either as a trophy or elegant meal, the first in a while. Ok!' The Game had been called upon, with a clear release but the time period was unknown.

Swallowing his breath as though it contained a drink. A gulp. Maybe a brief thought of resentment.

'Game, welcome back.'

'It's ok, John, now can we hurry this up I was in the middle of a sweet dream, them really erotic types.' Still always smiling, which puzzled me as to how he did it. Everything he said always tried to discomfort the other person within the conversation.

'Do you rape dead people for the same reason's as the living one's you tortured?' Straight and direct to the point, very unusual for John.

For dramatic effect, a long pause. Clapping hands, smiling sadistically , looking all around the room apart from at John. Now what was going on.

'Can't be bothered talking about this now, do you mind if I go? Not like you have any choice or say in the matter. Ha!'

'WAIT, just for one second,' John quickly responded before he exited the session.

The body with both personalities sat in limber as this man wanted to know an answer, as my personality just could not be bothered.

'Just one question please.' Through desperately begging the therapist sat.

'John no need to beg, it frankly makes you look as pathetic as you sound. I rape dead people, to finish or complete the task at hand which has been successfully performed to perfection by moi. Haha! A marker as such like any serial killer! Oh not forgetting a major factor, it just really, really turns me on. The arousal accomplished by it. You should try John! Improve your existence and possible put your, if any sex life into overdrive. Then again you need to be able to finish in your wife. I mean ejaculate without having to go to the shower with a shaven haven porn mag!!! Good answer? Don't matter! You need not answer now. Good Bye.' No longer just sat in limber . Now just back to Danny.

CHAPTER SEVENTEEN

Prior to the killings, having gained the information upon father and son also in the process been welcomed to a full time job through respect of mutual enemies which my parents need not know about. The message had also been delivered to the Johnson's. I was far into the apprenticeship now thanks to the knowledge passed down from Billy. However I still hadn't drawn up a plan or format nor acquired the knowledge of murder.

'Patience is a virtue that will bring great things.' Billy said to me one morning. Whilst in his company he just kept regularly looking at the time. Kind of hypocritical to use the word patience but he was the master and I was the apprentice. As he saw me he kept regularly looking at the time. 'If you want to go out and kill him, please don't let me stop you. However I really don't think you'll get very far in my honest opinion.'

A blatant statement with the thought of possible deception. The thought crossed my mind that I would get as far as his office door before I myself ended up dead. He had control of whatever was due to happen.

I remained seated. Curious as ever. Still desperately needed a personal plan in a subject I had no knowledge of. Nothing was been achieved this way, all I seemed to be as every passing day closed was nothing more than Billy's lapdog. I once heard the statement

' Why bark, when I have a dog to do it?' which remains a true moral to this very day.

The phone rang, Billy put the conversation strangely onto loud speaker.

'Hello Billy..' in a fearful, reserved almost boyish tone the man on the end of the line sounded.

'James, what a pleasure, just thinking about you, speak of the devil!! I believe you have something for me. How are profits?' No nonsense, straight to the point as Billy was not a time consuming person.

'Well, to be honest, it's a quiet time of year. I have your rent ready but a small percentage on the profit share which we agreed.'

Me again, Danny sorry. The man on the other end of the conversation was James if you haven't figured that out. I'm just here to comment before the conversation ends. A year back, James came to Billy with a business plan to open another strip club in the town as the other one was always full. However boredom of seeing the same product was causing a fall in retention.

James presented the plan, he had enough money to open, and start the business. However he was uncertain about any competition in the area so he sought after Billy's services to gain a loan. Billy looked at the plan and thought over it. He agreed on him putting the plan into motion however altering a few things such the market audience should be aimed at an upper market class. Keeping out scumbags, to serve high quality products at a slightly higher price to his first club, catering for doctors or lawyers etc..

James gladly excepted the deal. Billy drew up the papers, then signed them. Without thinking this man had his vision of a strip club called Curves. The agreement just signed between the two was not just for a loan. Billy had just bought into the business. Only a mere twenty five percent and collect tax returns and the profits quarterly.

As you would imagine it was a bumpy first for James but once he embraced his partner or investor, the party scene at the club increased upon a large unexpected scale. Not what, more who you know.

'James I personally don't visit often as I'm quite the busy man. Don't think you have a free pass or image to do as you please due to the fact every time those doors open one of my people will be there keeping a close eye on you, along with my earnings. The message here James, don't ever lie to me. I'll you put you in touch with our accountant. I'll collect tomorrow, understand, good!' Without allowing James to answer, he hung up the phone cutting off the connection.

'How do you know he'll have anything for you?' I asked, with a confused almost stupid look upon my face.

'If he does not well you receive a lesson in debt collection.'

Next night the club was closed for some unexplainable reason. A

Friday night, one of the busiest, lucrative nights of the week for any bar especially an erotic bar with a touch of elegance about the place.

'Open this God dam club, get the staff working, make the money lost , give the staff double pay for the shift explaining it as a bonus for all the messing around. You two find him and bring him to me. Now.'

Far from the happiest man in the world, I followed him towards the car, keeping any thoughts or comments to myself. That evening we collected all debts, taxes and rents owed from everything. After doing so, Billy returned to gym, opening a bottle of whiskey to have a glass providing a calming effect. He kindly offered me a glass. Not really a drink that agrees with me to be honest. I got a bottle of water from the fridge in the gym an alternative. Billy was not offended by my choice of drink. At least I would remain completely sober and focused for any task at hand, pleasing Billy highly.

'You are going to learn. You're going to learn how to kill at some point tonight. Ok.'

'Ok. Yeah.' Holding up my water as though it was a toast. Billy just smiled at me showing my enthusiasm. He found it amusing especially as to how the night was progressing.

'You do this right, the business is yours. Yeah, that's right the club will belong to you. Still my share would be taken off you quarterly.'

This was a lesson as a sense you don't screw this man over, or make deals with him however I was about to receive an up market strip club off him. What did I care.

An hour or so later, knocks on the door. A dark figure enters the room, the figure turned out be one of the men sent to find James.

'Got him. What we doing with him?' he asked subtly

'Take to the park. We will follow.' I was thrown a bunch of keys, looks like I was driving becoming the taxi driver.

The best thing about this town was it was full of country parks. Once night took over the skies, people abandoned the thought of using these areas. Teenagers even did not use them to get drunk at the weekend which is bizarre as it was a safe hold because the police don't check them. Going to a nearby park, I checked out the gates at the entrance to find out they actually opened without the use of a lock.

Going deep into the middle of the park the car in front of me just came to a halt. Pulling a man out of a back seat. Not tied up, or handcuffed just beaten as though a true pleasure was accomplished through what appeared to be a tragedy for the beaten sole.

'Why try and run with my money? Going anywhere nice with it? Did you think you would actually get far with it?..' A pause,

Coughing is all you heard and blood present in the outburst was all you could see and hear of the subject. A certainty was clear that this man was beaten to the panicle of death. If not treated shortly I am sure he would die of internal bleeding.

Not answering any questions, just coughing up blood and crying. What a pitiful creature. However all the man wanted at first was to open a competitor for the other strip club. The reason to stop a monopoly effect on the market in the town. Wrong. It all existed through Billy anyway, Ironic!!

'Is my money at your house? You know what to do..?'

The men around Billy just jumped on him like vulture's once again. Finished with that man.

'Stop,' I shouted, the man was still suited up, so walking up to him. I checked his pockets for wallets, money, I.D anything.

I found the wallet

'Pin code please,' was my question to the rising puddle of blood. Slowly but surely

'7986' dryly coughed out of his frail body.

'Sorry, one more time just a little slower and louder.'

'7,cough,9,pause,8 cough and the cheek of a pause 6' with a resistance in giving the final digit.

Handing over the wallet to Billy, nodding at my quick actions and showing common sense. They tried to help him back to his feet. Wavering in a slow circular motion, lymph in body structure or stance. Billy placed one of his punches upon him. Allowing gravity along with punch to push him towards the ground upon which he staggered. It still did not kill him. What resilience? In my opinion he should have stayed lay on the ground.

'So you have never killed a man Danny?' Looking at me with an evil glare.

Not ready for his question or prepared for this moment. I stepped back, pointing to my chest, speechless for the first time in a long time.

'Who? Me?.. No sir' I had a first row ticket to this onslaught but I found that amusing but never had I done anything close to that task.

'Well, son you're in luck. Tonight you receive your crash course in debt management recovery and the kill if non payment is the answer from the client. Now you are going to finish this simple task at hand set before you. How do you want to end it?' Not a care in the world. The man was no longer a threat nor would he be alive by sunrise anyway.

'Wait one second.' I walked back to our car. Opening the boot of the car. Filled like a toy box with practically anything that could be classed as harmful. This included a full petrol unit. I grabbed along with a sledge hammer for some unknown reason. A primitive weapon however it usually brought satisfaction to the Hench men. I walked back to the mayhem.

'Hahaha! You want to burn him, now what's the hammer for? Anything particular?' bringing a baffled looked to Billy and the others.

'Watch..' A simple response provided by myself.

Placing the canister my feet. Looking down at an almost life like creature. Shrugged my shoulders, showing I had no compassion for the man or matter at hand. Picked up the hammer. You would not believe the smile upon me at that very moment. Truly amazing it was.

I swung the hammer towards his toes. Followed by the hands. You could hear the crack, the anguish and pain as he screamed to the top of his voice, as it echoed around the baron park. The blood squirted out of his mouth even harder. At that point I stepped back making sure that none of it went on to me.

'That's not going to kill him.' One of the two men broadcasted expecting me to stand clear as they would continue the job at hand. Turning expressing anger. I thought right you want a murder watch this. I am a pure amateur. Ok! It's my first subject, but it was most certainly already dead.

Throwing the hammer into the air above, straight back down with the hope that it came with enough density to damage the lungs, the sound of the breaking rib cage multiplied with thunderous echoes.

'Hahaha! This is so much fun' I shouted to everyone.

'Yeah well get on with it as I have things to do.' Billy shouted at me.

Looking at him directly, showing the sincerity as he finished shouting. Games were coming to an end, I thought I best finish the task. Looking down at his red, bloody face surrounded by spatter in every direction. The hammer naturally swung at his teeth making sure he became unidentifiable, followed by his eye sockets then to finish that I crushed his pitiful head. Now he was completely finished. I was having the time of my life however I did have company, and it was rude to keep them waiting. Time for the finally to complete the show.

Turning back at Billy I said 'Ok, now time for the final piece of the killing.'

I poured petrol all over starting head down towards the toes. Anything that was traceable got covered in the flammable substance. Eventually the petrol can became empty. I stood back, then threw on a match, which I had contained in my pocket. I had a celebratory cigar but I'll save that for later.

My kill, pleasing Billy, my mentor. We got back in the car and drove back to the gym. This time I took a shot whiskey from Billy, accompanied by my cigar.

'You did well tonight. Well done. You just earned yourself a strip club. So here's to your success.' Now he held his glass a toast formation.

I joined in with complete bliss. I had learnt my lesson in such a short period. It was just amazing what had been taught to me. Still the design was far from in place to finish my revenge plan.

I was thinking of just asking Billy for the advice or maybe seeing if he knew someone to complete the job. That would defeat the whole game process. I had learnt, executed . Why back down now? Anyway now was the time for celebration. I had killed, my first lamb to the slaughter, as a payment for that task I received seventy five percent of a club. Excellent. Finally on the path to making money in which I rightly deserved.

The next day in the local paper. The headline. 'Man discovered burnt alive in a country park.' That was all they had. On the inside page was about the country park, and the rest was pure speculation. Who was this man? What was the motive behind such a grotesque onslaught? Will it happen again?

CHAPTER EIGHTEEN

'Helll...helll....'

Flashes of red light, the vision of the surrounding room getting brighter. The brightness of the light, intensifying, there it was clear as day. 3.13, The numbers just kept repeating, over and over again. Visions of 3.13 cocooned in a white shell.

'Hell.. Aaaaahhh..Hheeelll'

Something appeared to block the final digit, however it still remained. The numbers, an unidentified object. A hand, I'm not lying. As clear as day. Right before my eyes it was a thumb reaching out for the numbers.

'Hellll...ppppp'

The hand before me, with whatever vision that was occurring started to jerk. The whole arm reached out straight. Just jerking at a high intensity, with every available muscle tensing, pulling back and forth. This did not prevent the body to head for the numbers.

Besides the 3.13 been lit as a bright illumination the rest of the surrounding space was in complete darkness. A torturous event without the use of my legs, it most certain that I lay down.

3.15 Struck. My arm fell, just dropping as all control became unattainable for at least one second. Eyes shut allowing the darkness to take over, no more light or strobes of red. As calming as that sounds, the ordeal was far from over. Rolling onto my back, resting both shoulders securely on the bed beneath me. The body then had an explosive sensation run all the way through it. This time no numbers. Eyes completely shut, teeth bouncing up and down like a child on a bouncy castle. The tongue pushing forward as hard as it could, Every so often this meant be caught between the grips of the teeth, Squeezing, crushing like a steak knife straight through to tongue. Blood from what seemed to be the same wound, every time this happened, the wound got deeper, takings days if not weeks to heal. The neck arched following the direction of the lower spine and pelvic thrusts rocketing into the higher atmosphere, feet and hand pushing into the bed in which I lay.

Remaining in that position, the body once again shut down. Somehow, the brain sends electrical impulses to the muscles ordering the spasms to start.. For twenty minutes. It all starts with the first look of those digits. Eventually the morning after I realized it was my alarm clock in which I reached for.

With this happening all at once, the bed suffers an earth quake of power that would be simply off the Rictor scale. The bed only had this kind of action when I made love to a beautiful women. I'd personally say more hardcore sex, far from comforting or satisfaction.

It had to reach it's pinnacle, everything has a start and finish...Morning finally approached.

'Get your lazy arse!!!.... Out of that Fucking bed.' Mother shouts up the stairs. Five minutes later the replay of shouts happened once again suffering the wrath of a mothers tone.

'Well! Are you getting up today?' To make sure I heard her this time, she stood at the brink of the bedroom with one propping her stance upon the door frame.

'Well! To make you hear this, I said are you getting up?'

'Yeah..' Throwing arm in regrettably towards hers to acknowledge the fact I understood.
'Whatever, Yeah! If you want. I'll get up you cruel woman.' In a dreary unwanted tone. Cruel woman would not fit the description I had of her at this very moment, more a wicked witch, having the nerve to drag me out of bed. I am after all a young adult.

It was only 10.30am , it felt like dawn in my head. Most days I usually rise up around midday, What was so important, that I was dictated upon to get out of bed? Pushing myself to sit up inside the covers of the bed. Still stuck in a comatose dreary sleep. Arching forward, yawning. Staring at the clock as to the time, that could not be right. 10.30am, really. 10.30am In doing so I tried so hard to figure out the day that we were on. Confusion was now the strongest part of my mind. It is a Monday, maybe Thursday? I don't know no, hold on a second I'm sure I'll figure this puzzle out. That was it, the day was Saturday. Mother only arrived back home last night which just happened to be Friday.

Feeling sick as if I had actually got round to saturating a pub of its whole content. Rapidly the feeling reached the back of my throat, so it did not progress any further by actually going through the motions of been head first in a toilet. I swallowed any sort of back vomit waiting to exit my weakened body. Still a strong potent taste circled around, refusing to disappear of both vomit with the added bonus of I think blood. A true fact is that I did go to the pub last night. Knowing my boundaries of alcohol intake, after four pints of Carling larger and the possible odd shot of brandy to add the glamour in which I sort after, I called a taxi to take me home. The same taxi firm as usual, I had comfort in their reliability along with the way they always made sure I reached the destination as quick as possible. That they knew me so well, that when I rung all I had to do was say my name, they tell me the destination after that. Returning the question it was usually a reply of yes, as soon as possible please. Within five minutes the taxi pulled up outside the pub.

'Hello....Danny, Home?' the taxi driver asked in a happy tone, almost pleased to see me.

'Hello Mamu, Yes home sounds good, please. How are you Manu?' With the regularity using this firm, it was kind of difficult not to know the drivers by name as every driver brought a different conversation with every route taken. I was not going to return the favour with the rude gesture of not learning their names.

'Oh, I'm very well! Mr. Danny. How are you feeling?' with the tone or accent pronounced through the Muslim society he answered back.

'You already know Mamu, Same old shit, just different fucking day...! What could of changed since our last meeting.' As we both laughed showing the similarities within the middle class society.

So there it was, still having the feeling of sickness, just not a hangover. Every muscle in my body just ached all over, drained of any available energy. The neck, so tight, the pain stood out from the rest of the body. So tight that it cramped the head movements restricting the shoulders from doing their duties. Gradually through patience it released whatever control it had over me. Massaging the surrounding muscle tissue, of the trapezius allowing me to twist the neck. Still with fatigue the head had its normal rotations back. Although I'm writing this down,

I can't explain through word the simulation of how I actually or felt. The pain felt last night after going to sleep was unjustified.

Ten minutes later I actually managed to get down stairs, pushing myself into the kitchen. Unlike every other morning words were the last thing on my mind. Fatigue followed with immense hunger just ran all the way through me. Mother stood before me. Holding a brew for, a lovely most desired cup of coffee waiting for my arrival. Now that is motherly love. With an angry expression on her face as she passed the cup over to me, she did have an eerie sense of relief about her. A smile beginning to crack the surface of the hard faced motherly face she had about her. The relief she expressed was the fact that I had even woken up at all, let alone managed to walk to the kitchen with the hurdle of the stairs preventing such a cause. Her first born child was alive.

'Were you pissed last night?' Her first words as I stood before her. The tone of anger once again engulfing her vocal chords.

'No, as if. I know my boundaries when having a drink.' trying my hardest not to turn it into an argument or raise the tension before us both any further.

After having those brief words, turned my attentions towards where my medicine was. Every day to my knowledge this medication would be the most important part of my life. 700mg of epilium to be taken in the morning when I wake and in the evening before I go to sleep. Mother with eyes like a hawk, watching over to see if I actually took them. Surprisingly she did not ask me to open my mouth to check I had swallowed them. That did come as a shock!! Talk about trust! I suppose in a way it was only motherly love, showing she cared more than life itself.

'It happened again...' Mother stated the obvious as I finished the intake of medication.

'I know.' With my head down walking towards the sink to finish the task. making sure the tablets reached their destination, plus the last thing I wanted was a stray tablet stuck at the back of my throat.

'So you're positive you weren't drunk? Do you have any idea what caused it this time. Over twenty minutes it lasted, they are getting worse, I came in the room, to try and comfort you, making sure you did not swallow your tongue. I was scared to the point it actually brought me to tears, as I could do anymore than observe you. Nobody should have to see that let alone a mother watch her child go through the motions. So what are you actually doing to help or prevent all this from happening? Getting pissed every weekend and living off takeaways. I also heard you are practically drinking every day. Is that true?'

Swallowing any remaining water, I took the glass to the sink and washed it clean. Taking a minute from this whole conversation, I just stared into the sink. Having a numb tongue which made talking a struggle. The incision made throughout the seizure could be felt as the teeth gently rubbed against it trying to figure out the density and damaged caused. Struggling to think, drained causing a slight headache. Tears trying to leave my eye sockets, that was not going to happen on this occasion. My mother had seen enough, I could not allow her to see me so weakened by the events that the encore was me crying. Sniffing my nose as though I had the start to a common cold, blinking at the same time to wash away any tears formed. Then looked directly at her.

'I really don't know. I took my medicine. I've been taking it as regular as clock work. The drinking, well yes I drink regularly at home which is only a few bottles whilst watching a film or to relieve boredom. At the pub if I choose to go then well I stop within my limits. Mother had you not figured out that the condition has no on/off switch.' Honesty would be the only thing she would expect, so I gave it to her a simple as it could be put across.

My life is essentially ruined. I'm not allowed into night clubs in case I have a weird reaction towards the strobe lights. However it's a very small percent that it would happen. Still not worth the risk or embarrassment upon my behalf. I'm most certainly not allowed to drink, however I do look past all the know all on that subject. If I fancy a beer then I'll have one. The mind of a young person entails that life should be fun before settlement of marriage, family life happens to them. Everything I had encountered so far apart from the relationship with Sarah was a dream or fantasy. When things get so bad or stress begins to takeover in any part of my life it triggers a seizure within my sleep.

Shame really, however I have a little more to express that doesn't entail the seizures. So please take the time to reach the end.

CHAPTER NINETEEN

There she lay right before my eyes. Angelic would be a cheap rip off and a very poor metaphor for the beauty that glowed from her essence. Holding a smile tenfold with the size of the Eiffel tower. Long, soft hair with a slight bounce flowing down towards her shoulder. A strand fell lose covering one eye, not enough to shadow the face. Speaking of the eyes, they looked towards the ceiling in a distracted vision that could only be described as…me.

'Are you coming to bed?' followed by a sweet giggle, describing the innocence yet the naughtiness waiting to escape the girl that was… No other girl worthy of time or the love greater than universe I felt for her. Of course there right before my stance lay Sarah.

On the bed she was right before me yet still dressed as was I. Unusual circumstances at this point for any girl been laid upon the bed asking at that very question. I looked back around the room, then prior to answering Sarah's question, something else struck the attention of myself.

In less than thirty seconds the numbers glimmered three one three. Three one three for a second time, both in red. Four times I encountered those very numbers with one minute. Then it flickered to the following sequence three one four. I still stood without jerking, yet how did I see those numbers so frequently in such a small period of time. A seizure would last a hell of a lot longer. Sarah interrupted my thought process.

'Are you coming to bed or not? I'm getting very tired, Well are you?' Impatience growing vastly in her tone. 'Fine, Don't expect anything in the morning or when we wake, if I'm still here. Most unlikely. You better not wake me when you do decide to get in bed. Your fucking loss. Night!' Grabbing the covers as she rolled away from my attention. I presume once she calmed, she would go to sleep.

For that brief moment in time what was so important about that distraction that was not a seizure? It happened again with three one five, only the repetitions grew faster, again not with the side effects of a related seizure. What was actually going on.

From the bed I turned away looking whilst thinking what was running through my mind to cost a romantic, lustful end or beginning of two souls interacting. Right before my eyes shone the numbers clear and bright as the sun rising with a golden glamour. Reaching out the right arm towards the distraction with complete control of the situation without recurring muscle jerks. Too far away to gain access over the number yet close enough to read. The numbers not repeating within the mind at the pace I previously thought.

Lowering the arm by my side stepping towards the red intense light. Placing the left arm just above the numbers. Red shinning through the fingers, around the hand, still not enough of the colour to fill the room. So I returned the arm back to beside my standing leg. Flashing once more The numbers continued to repeat at the same rhythm, confusing myself.

I had been drinking that was a fact that could not be denied. Not enough to be drunk, or close to legless. Joyful the most suitable description at the moment in question. Turning around placing the right hand across the forehead contemplating the possible outcome, or reasons for what was actually happening. The numbers appears right before my eyes, yet I had turned away from them. In fear I stepped back reaching out for anything to hold onto. A shelf came into my possession, turning to make sure it was stable yet safe. The numbers continued to and reflect before me, there was no escape. Trapped, concealed, controlled by the repetition of an ongoing code. I'm positive it was not a seizure. I have no sense of time or continuation during that horrible occurrence.

Once more I focused all my attention to Sarah. Far from a distraction, still she lay with a cute smile as she dreamt. A beautiful rose in bloom she was. The moment I started to watch her sleep with such innocence my distractions of recurring numbers disappeared. With peacefulness as she slept I placed my thumb gently on to her cheek. Softly I moved away the lost and stranded hair concealing her eye, that stole her attractiveness by taking away her face. Once doing so, I realized what I had lost by not getting in bed with her when asked to. Now without any other reason to join her apart from the warmth and security having her lay in my arms. I decided it would the best to get undressed and get to lie with her asleep or not. Bliss it would be.

I stood completely to get undressed, directly facing the window to destroy any fears or doubts of going to sleep. Focusing the eyes towards the window caused the numbers to appear from both directions in either eye. That direction getting undressed only made things worse.

It had to stop, there and then. Why would it not stop? A seizure would cause great panic to Sarah through the noise and actions that would happen. Right I turned to once again face the numbers head on. I closed my eyes as I thought it must be a dream. A horrific dream or nightmare trying desperately to ruin the best thing that ever happened in my life. I will not allow anything to come between me and Sarah, in eternity we shall remain.

Upon opening my eyes, the familiarities of also seeing my reflection. I could not have drank that much to forget the mirror that hung above the bed. Of course the mirror caused the confusion. Shaking my head! Thinking that stupidity was the only thing that described my thoughts. Madness.

I took the t-shirt off opposite the mirror to watch myself get undressed. Upon doing so I recognized every healing wound, scratch and scar that had happened through mostly past seizures. I don't believe for one second that seizures throughout my life were caused through lack of sleep, alcohol abuse, or stress preaching its breaking point. A mental condition causing so much bodily harm with due cause. A natural punishment to add to mishaps and accidents that occur every day.

Wearing a pair of jeans that fell below the waistline held up by a belt that struggled holding them in place. Calvin Klein label in black and white appearing above the belt buckle. Above that a pale body, with a growing six pack although not completely sure as to the cause of image. Was the reasoning of the six pack due to exercise or the diet that provided myself with the build or lack of.

Finally I took a glance or it could have been described as a long thoughtful stare with empty thoughts producing no results to the unanswered questions. What just happened?

The tongue gently rubbing along my teeth at it reached its destination, pushing out the upper right lip in escape of the mouth, in circular motion repeating the same action upon the lower lip. The right hand rubbed in a downward motion from the nose, covering the whole lower half of the face. It continued its course downwards until the thumb softly but firmly encountered the finger.

121

Staring right into my reflection, would that answer any questions or doubts. My eyes directly parallel of course reaching deep into my own thoughts seeing only myself. Pupils completely dilated not due to the drink incurred, something else.

Ever growing. The light just expanding destroying the image in which I had personally sought after. The heavier the light grew the whirlwind that was the pupil dilation disappeared. The thoughts disappeared, the reflection gone. As was any memory of life to date. This was not a blackout, seizure or anything associated with the epilepsy. A blink, deep breath whilst grabbing the forehead to guarantee reality along with complete control.

A parallel existence it was far from that. Real it was. An ego most definitely not we had already discovered that reasoning. Feeling along with muscle control was still a part of my abilities. Now what was going on. Twenty five was the current age I felt but it was not to be

'Mummy, Mummy, it happened all over again, it really did. .All the same as before.'

Sitting shouting out those very words. Not in the same room. This was different, familiar yet different. Complete darkness, waking in a bed alone. Yet I had not gone to bed. I stood watching my reflection. How have I ended up here? What is to happen next? I know if it similar to the ego representation, then I should see out the ending and reason as to why. This will be the one and only answer I'm sure of it. Right I'm going to do it.

'What happened this time? Were you attacked by Freddie again?' mother replied whilst gently rubbing her hand across my forehead, encouraging me to go back to sleep as dreams can't hurt me.

'No not Freddie, I know that's not real. It was that man I have never seen but keeps talking to me. He says he is me.' Panicking, thinking the voice within would hurt me, grabbing the quilt fearful of the night or sleep.

'Go to sleep. I promise nothing will hurt you, I won't let them.' She guided me towards the bed, placing my head against the pillow after she pulled up the quilt tucking me in. Overseeing that I did actually go

122

back to sleep.

Waking up the following morning forgetting about the dream, as the rest of the night was peaceful, whilst relaxing. Going downstairs for breakfast I saw my mum. Making my breakfast, my favourite, beans on toast. As she placed the hot plate upon the table warning me to be careful as the plate would be very hot, for a little man like me. Something about her had changed, this was not the woman who scared off any bad dreams last night. Her face was puffed up on one side. Her upper lip had a red scar as one half popped out further than the rest. On the side her eye was purple with bits of yellow.

'What happened mummy? You hurt?'

'No, mummy Is ok, she just had a slight accident, nothing for you to worry about. Now eat your breakfast otherwise you will grow hungry later.' rubbing my head messing up my hair.

'Can I see daddy before I go to school?' with a folk filled with beans I gazed at her whilst asking that question.

'No, son. Daddy is sleeping, best not to wake him. You know the rules, when daddy is sleeping we let him sleep and don't disturb him. Now eat up and afterwards go clean your teeth ready for school. Remember don't wake your dad.' At the point before shouting yet her voice slightly raised from the calming one she had whilst serving breakfast.

Silently I crept round that house trying not to disturb or wake up my dad. I get shouted at if I wake him up before he has to get up. I don't like getting in trouble off him, it makes me cry sometimes. Maybe he makes mummy cry if she wakes him up.

When I finished school that day, we had art as one of the lessons. I drew a picture for dad especially. It was a picture of me and him in the park holding hands whilst the sun was shining. I ran into the house, all excited shouting my voice, holding out the picture ever so proudly.

'Daddy, daddy! I drawn this for you, daddy. Mum where's dad, I've got a present for him?' again ever so proud I held the picture to show her.

123

'He is not here, he's at the pub. I think. He'll be home later, you can give it at teatime. That will be a nice treat for him.' Again showing a smile, yet she struggled as the mouth was bruising as well. The eye grew no better.

Who and what had done that to my mother? For a child to see her mother, the strongest protector in the whole world weakened and bruised hurt me. I wanted to cry.

Later that night roughly around nine o'clock both me and my brother were sent to bed as per usual, and keeping with motions we showed great resistance.

'Now, both of you bed. I'm not asking, I'm telling you, bed.'

She was most definitely serious about the subject at hand. We were also threatened with a slapped bottom if we did not go to bed. I don't actually believe she would of done it, but I was not going to call her bluff.

At bedtime, dad still had not returned from where ever he had been. Another day had passed and I had yet to see my own father, my idol. This was the true reason as to wanting to stay up past bed time, I wanted to show him the picture of us in the park. Get his approval and gratitude of thinking of him as my favourite person. I'm not quite sure if it was a male thing but it just seemed natural to choose my father over my mother as the statue to idolise, the masculinity that I could possibly be some day. I would be as strong and manly as he was. That was the dream anyway.

After going to bed, we were tucked in by mother, as she said goodnight she left the room turning out the light in the process. So there it was the end of that day or so I thought. A couple of hours later I heard shouting, angry tones including screams. Sometimes mother would shout in anger at me and my brother but it was not a female voice shouting that voice appeared to be screaming in return to something. The whatever noises we close by, almost next door but with a little more distance. As many times I have heard screams and bangs from the room of my parents. These noises that woke me were far from the same or similar. Through insist as well as curiosity I had to find out and see for myself what was causing these noises. If I was awake it only natural so was my brother. I saw in him the corner of my eye. Scared and trembling with the covers towards his chin as he sat with tears flowing.

'Wait here ok. Don't worry I'm going to find out what it is. I promise it's nothing to be scared of. Try and go back to sleep, ok. Whatever you do don't leave your bed or this room.' I tried so hard to comfort him, and encourage him back to sleep, yet in all that time the noises continued.

I wandered all around the top of the house, there was nobody around, I checked my parents room last and that was also empty. It was not that room that echoed the screams.

I gently stepped down the stairs trying not to be heard as I would get in trouble if I was found downstairs after bedtime. Pushing the living room door open, with every inch showing immense and utter carnage. The image of the aftermath left after a robbery. A chair pushed over. The table top broken all the way through, a picture of the whole family lay smashed upon the carpet. The noises continued to get louder with the female tone becoming the dominant of the two. It all been expelled from the kitchen if it was in our house, it was the only place left and most logical answer. The mess of the room was another matter that I could think about some other time. I followed the path towards the kitchen trying not to be heard myself whilst doing so trying ever so hard not to step on anything that could cause my harm such as broken glass. That would be painful, and then I would run the possibility of been caught out of bed.

At the kitchen edge I stood, peering my head into it trying not to be seen, I tried to hide within the shadows as such. The noises were erected from this very room. My mum and dad were having a mass argument that was out of this world.

'Listen you stupid bitch. I don't have to explain anything to you. I never have and never will. If I want to go the pub, bookies then it's my fucking choice, not yours. I'll do as I want to, not what you want me to do, are you listening to me, my fucking life.'

To make sure he had control the argument and that she took in all that he said, he cracked his hand right across the side of the recently bruised face. That was a noise more frightening than that horror film. The intensity of the blow drove my mother sideways falling over the sink. Before she had time to react to his comments or beating, he grabbed her by the arms prevent any sort of retaliation. After doing this, he shook so hard…

'Yes, yes, I understand…ye, yes' in a tired response to his questions. It was far from over. The onslaught continued. I was unsure as to what started the questioning or brutality into the argument but my father was making his point. It was physically made as well as ever so loudly heard. It just echoed. There was nothing rhetorical in his questioning. Just pure Neanderthal apex brutality.

'Just what the hell gives you, the fucking right to ask stupid questions? Do you actually believe your better than me, or have some power over me. Wow! We have kids, so tell me something new. Don't forget those two little shits are not the only kids I have. For all you know I could have seen my other children today. But no you have already drawn your conclusions. Well now I'm going to show you mine.'

His arm swung right back towards her face this time his hand was fisted to provide more damage on impact. Then after doing this he pulled her back from the sink once again he continued to beat her, but not at the face anymore. He continued his beating around the ribs, and stomach. Once tiring out, of pulling her back and forth from the sink, he pulled her away from that then threw her towards the floor face first.

I stepped back making sure I was not to be seen. I did not like what I witnessing but what could I have done. An eight year old child covered in tears stood watching his mother been tortured by his father.

Once on the floor, I presumed this whole ordeal had reached its end, I even thought it was a nasty dream. He kicked her with such density causing blood to spatter out in all directions. I did not want to be seen or caught now, so I snuck under the kitchen table remaining hidden. I could still see everything. I lay in fear, crying, trying not to make a sound, although at this point it would not have made a difference. He was making all the noise.

After the swift small beating provided by my father, he reached for the fridge pulling out a cold bottle of beer. He stood beside her watching her cry and bleed. All his doing, he stood drinking as though it was a well deserved celebratory drink to toast his masculinity. The trophy was secure. She spat out any remaining blood that had become present, arising to her feet, head back, her stance folding out to defend her side of the argument.

'Have you finished? Is that the best you've got? You are a worthless waste of space. I should have listened to everyone when they said don't marry you. You're a cockroach, A stupid vermin like bastard. Absolutely nothing. You actually believe constant beatings would make me beg for your approval? By the way they are not stupid little shits as you put it. Those two children are beautiful creatures that I don't know how, are unfortunate to contain your D.N.A. Those two children are the only reason our marriage has lasted this long.' Now her argument stood as proud as she did.

I lay watching this torment. What to feel, or was there any thing that could be done? Too young to help or get involved or truly understand the actual meaning of the situation. How it started or would it eventually finish its course? Eventually it would succeed to have a damping effect upon everything. This I was certain, even for an eight year old I understood something as drastic as that been observed had no happy outcome.

He actually laughed. Threw his bottle towards the door which held the door fame. I'm glad I took shelter under the table.

'You call that a fucking answer. You thought that pitiful crack answer would somehow offend me or hurt me? You are a really stupid fucking slag. All these threats of ending the marriage or the only reason as to me been in this family. Wake up! They are empty as you are. Repeating shells of threats. You don't have anywhere to go, if you left. You can't support yourself or those kids. They would not be left with me.'

'Do you really think I'd let you have them. The most valuable assets in my world. I can't believe your arrogance. You're the thick minded one. I would risk life and limb for those children. You can't support yourself, how would you raise two children. I know you haven't seen your other kids in a very long time. Nor do I believe you'd give up drink or bookie time. HELL NO! I wouldn't trust you or see capable of raising them.'

Crack, once more this time making sure she hit the floor with an impact. Then once again he kicked her multiple times, as before the blood started to flow out of her. He went back to fridge, opened another bottle.

'What the fuck are you going to do this time? You have got a whole house to clean up before those special kids of yours get up.' Kicking her once more.

'I'll tell you what I'm going to do.' Once again rising to her feet, standing toe to toe with my father. She spat blood all across his face, followed by a slap leaving a red mark upon the skin bracing the blunt of the impact. This was a proud moment for my mother as the battle was turning in her favour.

This did not amuse my father, touching his lower lip looking to see if it caused any form of bleeding. Whilst still holding on to the precious bottle, as I doubt he would of wasted this one. He gripped the bottle fiercely around the top. Before any words could be spoken from any party. The bottle swung in the direction of mothers forehead. Smash, straight over her face, as beer mixed with the open wounds as glass shattered everywhere.

She screamed, grabbing her face and quickly turning away to hide any dignity left within the empty mother of a shell. Completely turned away from him now with only her back to him. Now it was to come to an end, my father kicked her at the back of the knee caps forcing her in only one direction, the floor. He grabbed a handful of hair pulling her weakened body and distilled face so his expression could be witnessed.

'You stupid cow, Like I said if I want to go to the pub then I will. Now clean this fucking mess up.' Pushing her down. Face first. Now another beer had been wasted, he grabbed another whilst looking all round the fridge.

'Damn! Last one. You better get some more beer in tomorrow since you've wasted most of these, we've none left now. I'm going bed, see you in the morning.'

He walked past her, but not before stepping over her to reach the kitchen exit. Turned back towards where she lay, shook his head, shrugged his shoulders then walked towards the bedroom.

As the living room door slams shut, followed by bangs along the stairs, I turned my attentions towards my mother getting slowly up. She

128

covered in blood like she just had a long bath. Red was the color in which she stood. Crying out the pain and confused as to what had just happened? Grabbing her head, looking down on her now bloodied hand, weary of how she was able to stand. If an eight year old understood the word concussion that would have been my conclusion, however I didn't.

'Mum, are you ok?' crying just as bad as she was however mine more fear than actual pain. Staring at her seeing the hostility expressed right before my eyes and used upon this caring figure so important to me.

'Daniel. What are you doing out of bed? How long have you been down here? You know you should never be down here after bedtime.' Still expressing more concern for me than herself. She needed medical attention, I personally did not know this and even if she did I don't think she'd get them involved.

'Why did Daddy do this to you? Are you ok?' Watching her wiping her head.

'Mummy is fine. Now go back to bed. You never saw any of this. Ok? This is our little secret, just me and you.' That was an order, not an excitable secret for an eight year old to conceal. She gently embraced my shoulder encouraging me back to back. Had better reasons in my life to ushered to bed.

'Good night. Go on back to bed' What else could I have done. I gave her a hug then continued back to bed, still with gentle tears in my eyes.

The next morning getting up for school, going downstairs to check on mother. Breakfast was waiting for us both. She stood over us by the sink cigarette in one hand, smoke leaving her mouth, with one side hidden away from us facing the window. Slight reflections showed the damage caused but not to the full intensity. Dad was still asleep, no doubt still drunk and dreaming of his actions.

Scenes like this were a common occurrence within the house, however never until today was an explanation given. Mother always gave an excuse to protect her and the image we had of father. The pain and suffering put upon her, and she expected this punishment to make sure we saw a nice family, happy home. That makes no sense to me as an adult. As a child I knew no different.

The images shown to myself by the fatal accident watching the brutality or tragedy always made me cry when thinking about them. Mother came to me after breakfast.

'Now what did I say last night about what you saw?'

'It was our secret, and I was not to tell anyone.' I stood once again almost in tears. My mother in that state and the image of my idol destroyed through such horrific events.

'Good boy, now finish getting ready for school, make sure you clean your teeth. I'll check, and I will know if you haven't.' trying ever so hard to smile whilst saying that to me.

Nightmares began to follow after seeing that beating. Night after night it haunted me. If it caused me sleepless nights I tried to imagine what my mother thought about. A child at my age seeing those images began to batter me inside, hurting without actual physical harm.

One Friday a few weeks later, me and brother returned home for the weekend all excited. The abuse that I witnessed had sunk into my head slowly but surely I was forgetting all about. My mother had two tickets for the football match the following day. This meant only one of us was going. My brother was football mad, I personally never found an interest in it. So it was only fair he was to have it. I later found out that my mum will be accompanying the victor to this ticket.

'Will I be spending the day at grandma's then mum?' Showing further excitement as I would get to see grandma and granddad. It was rare we saw them as they lived quite far away in another county.

'No, dear you're going to spend the day with your dad.' my eyes just glazed over causing a distant look upon my face. Every vision from that night just flooded back into my head.

'No, I don't want to, I want to spend it with grandma and granddad. Dad is mean and cruel. I have seen it when he hurt you. ' trying ever so hard to show my unwillingness in doing so expanding my resistance. A whole day with a man who had no desire to spend it with me. His own

130

son, flesh and blood.

'Look, you're spending it with your dad and you have no choice in the matter. I don't know what you're talking about, dad hurting me. That is a nasty thing to say, so I never want to hear things like that again, otherwise you'll get a smack. Now for saying that daft thing, you're not watching T.V tonight, go to your room until tea then afterwards back there to continue your punishment.'

It happened, it was not a nightmare. Why would my mother punish me for saying it out loud. The conspiracy to cover up the event, even protecting the evil expressed through the hand of my father. No matter the punishment I was not looking forward to the next day. Where would I end up? I wondered as to what would happen to me if I was naughty. The night just seemed endless. I just tossed and turned constantly rolling over trying to close my eyes. I just could not do it, every time I did, flashbacks happened with different variations as to that nasty image. Tears along with hot sweats rolling off my innocent scared body.

An arm pulled on mine interrupting the thoughts been processed at that very moment.

'Are you coming to bed? You have been stood in front of that mirror for almost an eternity or at least that's what it feels like. Come on, come to bed with me and keep me warm.' Sarah softly spoke distracting the whole vision.

Snapping and pulling the arm off me, then something I have done. After the arm I pushed Sarah straight into the bed, raising my hand in a fist position so it drew parallel with my shoulder. I was about to hit her.

'God, are you not asleep yet? I'll come to fucking bed when I'm ready, you got that? Fucking hell..' Lowering my arm, decreasing the tone of anger that just expelled out of my mouth and directed straight at Sarah. A situation that was not needed.

At this point Sarah lay looking upwards at me, scared. She didn't return any gesture or abuse to complete what could have been an explosive situation. We were both over intoxicated, I she think she believed it was nothing.

'Sorry.' She gently rolled over with her head facing in the opposite direction to me, however sill remaining in the bed. After a minute or two later I watched over her as she went to sleep.

What had just happened? I nearly hit the love of my life in an unnecessary rage. I was more scared than her. Stepping back absorbing the past event, thinking of the possible harm that could of come from all that. The mirror still remaining in place. I turned my attention back towards it, this with guilt been the only thought of the moment. I just went over and over the thinking that was my childhood but it just would not return to the forefront of my mind. Drunk and just about to raise my arm towards my girl friend. I appreciated the fact I didn't.

Glamorized by my own reflection trying so hard to go back towards my childhood, the only thing that appeared were those stories I have already told. The stories which only came to light when I was in a seizure. Was it possible for the first time I was having a blackout. Just having a standing seizure where no muscles spasms just the complete glazed over appearance. It was very possible and not uncommon with epileptic seizures however unlikely with myself. They have only taken place during my sleep. Harm was only ever put on myself not others.

The stories just rotated clear as day on repeat. I'm positive if I wanted to return to one it would of happened. I stopped thinking for a brief moment turning around to look at the clock, and the time was completely different as to when we first arrived in the bedroom. Half an hour must of passed and yet there I stood fully dressed. It was far from a seizure. I had to figure this out.

Returning to the image that was my reflection taking deep breaths. This, whatever it was, had to end. Sarah was not going to come to any harm by the wrath of myself. Suddenly the mind brought back the image of the child.

Morning came about, I had finally got to sleep but I don't believe it was much. My brother running around the room shouting out his favourite football team, expressing excitement as though they were already the victors. In doing so he had no sense of guilt awaking me.

'Come on, get up.' fully dressed in the football shirt, and scarf around his neck.

He had the fortunate luck of spending the day with mother whilst I had the day with dad. Great! Slowly getting out of bed, got ready for the day at hand.

'Now you have Daniel for the day, you better look after him. It's not a very hard task as after all your son. It might do you good to spend some quality time with him.' Gracing her opinions upon him.

'Ok, yeah, yeah go to the fucking football. I'll look after that one. What time you due home to have him back?' whilst putting a cigarette in his mouth, it was a roll up so I imagine most of the conversation his attention was elsewhere.

'What time I give him back? He is not a fucking chore, treat him with respect, oh try to stay away from the pub or bookies. He has seen enough of you in drunk states.' Once again broadcasting anger in a raised tone.

'What the fuck do you mean he has seen me in enough states? What the fuck are you talking about? Fucking stupid bitch.' Raising his voice.

'Nothing we are going to be late, so treat him right, and I'll see you both later.' kissed him on the cheek then myself. Leaving the room along with my brother off for a day of enjoyment.

'You alright son, what you do want to do today with your dad? Anything exciting?'

Nothing came to mind. I just stood there struggling my shoulders in confusion to the questions asked of me.

'Well it doesn't really matter as what you want to do as your spending the day with me, and you're not interrupting my plans.' inhaling his cigarette looking at me as though I was some kind of disappointment or brick holding him back.

He left me stood there for a second as he went to the kitchen, a moment later he returned with a can in his hand. Special brew I think, it must have been a beer as I was never allowed to drink any. Breakfast had not long gone and yet there he stood drinking his first beer of the day. This was far from the last either.

'Don't worry son, the first race starts at twelve, so we will be going to daddy's playground in a minute, so go get ready if you're not already.' Race wonder what he meant by that, and parents had playgrounds, that sounded quite good to me.

After leaving the house he took me to place known as the bookies. I'm sure, my mother said we were not to go there but that hasn't stopped him so far. There were horse races on loads of televisions, and men stood in front of them waving tickets, shouting these horses to come on. It was a horrible place to be in. Men all round making all this noise surrounded by smoke letting off an essence so dreadful it made me constantly cough. I was punished for been there, my father placed me in a corner where he could still see but told me to wait there and not to move. For most of the day he continued to shout at the screens, then go back and forth to the windows with people behind them. Sometimes he got money back.

At about three o'clock he approached me.

'Well I don't know about you but daddy is very thirsty do you fancy a drink?' After been stood in the same corner for most of the day been punished for something I hadn't done. I had to reply yes, I had no real choice.

He took me to a pub. I am eight years old. I've spent most of the day with a father who only cares about himself going gambling, then with any winnings or remaining money now a pub to drink. Maybe they had cans of special brew in here.

'Right, I'll have a pint of Stella and you better get him a pint of orange juice to keep him quiet love.' Smiling at the bar maid as he passed over a ten pound note, trying so hard to attract the attention of this young girl with a hope of gaining something more than been served. He failed and I'm positive it wasn't the first or the last time. I hate rejection at the best of times, so why he would continue his quest is a great puzzle to me.

He handed me the orange, then tried to walk away.

'I'm hungry, I want something to eat. Can I have something to eat dad? Please.' Looking at him showing innocence whilst sadness as I really was hungry.

'God! You've just got a drink and now you want something else. Your just like your fucking mother. Barmaid have you got some crisps for him?'

'Yes, what flavour would you like? Salt and vinegar, prawn cocktail, cheese and onion, bacon fries?'

'Daddy, can I have some bacon ones.' Pulling on his leg in mere desperation hungry for the food.

'Fine give him the bacon ones. This is all your having till your tea, understand, now how much do I owe you?' looking back at the bar maid as though he had done some worthy good deed. She didn't see it that way as she replied with the straightest face.

'Fifty pence.' No please, just holding out her hand expecting payment, almost snatching it off him then walking away from him.

Dad then practically dragged me towards the gambler. He was known in the pub yet nobody spoke to him and he made no effort to communicate with anyone. A man well known yet stood in complete solitude. What a life to live. He avoided all family showing no grace or compassion all for this.

'Sit on this stool, don't move, speak to anybody or disturb me unless its urgent ok.'

Dragging the stool directly beneath me, then forcing me upon it. Turning away to face the gambler. Placing pound after pound into. Constantly pressing buttons. Yelling at it, slamming down upon its keyboard. These things didn't stop him. When he ran out of money he returned back to the till to get more change. Time went by so slowly, he just kept going back and forth to get change or fill his glass. An ever growing smell of beer and smoke gathering not just on him but the room itself. Around tea time, we still remained in the pub as after the football it started to get really busy. This didn't disturb my father in any shape or form. His anger just kept rising though.

'Dad, its tea time, are we going home?'

'What did daddy tell you? You sit there be quiet and don't bother me. So sit down and shut up. We'll go home when I'm ready to not you.'

Pushing back downs the stool with a greater force than before, he was mad and it was becoming more scary.

Three. One. Five, Three. One . Five, Three. One. Five. In a complete line, all flashing bright red. On a continuous loop. It wasn't a seizure. The images, the numbers kept appearing in a bright red colour with bells alongside them ringing and ringing. Another noise alongside them getting louder with different tones. The whole sequence lasted over a minute. The gambler had released its jackpot. Making noise and flashes to make it aware this machine had just become an empty one.

'Fucking yes, fucking too right!!' Dad shouting at the machine, he had won. Most of the day if not all spent wasting money he did not really have gambling and drinking ignoring the fact his son was beside him all that time.

Twenty five years those numbers have haunted me. The constant reflections appearing throughout my life. The red, the numbers. A constant reminder of the worst part of my childhood. A destructible force towards his whole family showing his only true love was in fact some of the worst addictions on the planet. Those addictions will slowly eat away at him destroying the environment within. I believe he didn't care as he enjoyed this lifestyle, living everyday as it came.

Those flashing lights shown when I was a child, presenting themselves when stress arose in myself. They were nothing more than reflections of the past, showing nothing could be worse than that time.

Dad I will admit hatred will always lie within my mind, heart and soul in remembrance of the way you treated your and my loving family. As will the fact that cannot be removed is dad I will always… undeniably love you. However you look or take that statement I guarantee even promise you, please listen to this. Look at me eye to eye if you ever see me again, stand as the man you believe you are, face to face look at me. I refuse to be you. I will grow old inheriting your ways or habits as you live your life. How you chose addiction over love is strange and unforgivable. I may have considered forgiveness however you chose not to contact me on either my 18th or 21st birthday, not by card or phone call, I know you have those details.

Once I saw the moment that fist rise to assault Sarah, it all became clear to me. You taught me these ways. It wasn't through intention as you were never sober enough to teach yourself let alone your child. Looking into the mirror, half blacked out, shadowing one side of the face. Dad that is you. Shining ever so bright the face of me. My reflection shows exactly as I want it, as it will grow into when that shadow is dissolved . With you now forgotten, peace will finally enter my sleep and unconscious mind. Upon reflection, I will never turn into what you are. My reflections shows I will stand only as myself.